Flash 40: Life's
Moments

Janelle Jalbert

ISBN Number: 978-1-942535-04-1 (eBook)
ISBN Number: 978-1-942535-05-8 (Paperback)

Synchron8 Publishing
www.synchron8publishing.com

Cover art by Samantha Hensler at ebookcoversgalore.com

Thank You!

We hope you enjoy *Flash 40: Life's Moments* and appreciate your support and readership of our initial installment of the Flash 40 series. Our goal is to follow up Life's Moments with other collections of flash literature, both fiction and memoir, in the future.

As a thank you, we at Synchron8 Publishing have a free bonus for you. Janelle has provided additional stories, not included in this collection, for readers of *Flash 40* to enjoy. Please take a moment to visit:

www.sychron8publishing.com/F40MomentsBonus

It is our way of saying…thank you!
To learn how you could be the next Flash 40 author,
visit the final pages of *Flash 40: Life's Moments.*

Table of Contents

Introduction

Flash 40: Life's Moments

Sure, life is full of defining moments. Births, weddings, new experiences, and deaths are easily viewed as turning points that shape lives. What about those other moments? The childhood memories, the wishes come true, and near misses that serve as touchstones for a life well-lived. *Flash 40: Life's Moments* explores the variety of beginning, middle, and ending events that define a life. These situations are both monumental and seemingly mundane.

Beginnings

How do you define a beginning? It may seem like an obvious question, yet the start of something new may not always be seen in traditional ways, depending on your vantage point. Birth is the beginning of one's life, but as the characters in "Can You Believe It?" learn, the birth of a child can be a beginning for all of those involved. Adopting a new family member is seen as an active pursuit by the person seeking the addition, but "Adoption Day" turns the tables on that notion.

A typical beginning hints at the promise of what's to come. However, that promise may not lead to immediate success as the driver in "Career Day" and the new bride in "Awkward" come to understand.

Seeing the world anew is also part of the process of initiation. That freshness can be the result of a new start as the characters in "Baby Steps" and "Home" experience. It can also be part of the voyage of discovery as Calen finds out in "Bucket List", or it could be the moment that you see yourself in a whole new light like Terri does in "A Model Discovery".

Middles

While everyone loves to begin fresh and new, most of one's life is spent amidst the day-to-day grind. Let's face it; there are more days in the middle of week than there are in weekends or the dreaded Mondays. What do those Tuesdays, Wednesdays, and Thursdays look like?

Some middles are wonderful experiences that spark lifetime memories which are fondly remembered down the road. Find out about the power of birthday waffles in "Birthday Wish" and the comfort of an "Old Faithful" as childhood experiences.

Some middles are lessons or tests of one's will. In "No Good Deed", Sharon learns that being responsible can have a messy downside. Marvin finds victory in "Lightning Fast" despite uncontrollable and crippling circumstances, but an "Addiction" creates a different challenge for a woman obsessed with a frozen dessert. For Trisha and Sylvie in "The Girl Code" a lesson about friendship becomes a bitter pill to swallow.

Some moments amid the daily grind are quirky gifts from the universe in the name of synchronicity, serendipity, and downright comedy. Finding love can be both a messy and disappointing endeavor as Kathleen in "Captain Meatball" and Tim in "Love in the Time of Online Dating" come to understand.

Traveling can enlighten those everyday moments, but a state trooper gets an unexpected surprise in the early morning darkness when he finds a "Rabbit". An unlikely appearance on the beach provides an entertaining detour for one couple's honeymoon in "Gorilla in Our Midst", while family dynamics keep things interesting in "Vacation Splash".

And then again, some middles are simply a pause or a fleeting moment in time. An "Awakening" occurs over a cup of coffee. Lance comes to understand when it's time to let go in "She Did It for You". Old acquaintances come to know each other again in "Genie in a Bottle". A simple question leads to bigger issues for a student in "Quota", and the character of a man is reflected beyond his time on earth in "A Dollar Matters".

Endings

Have you gotten accustomed to endings that are either happy or sad? Find out how endings may be more about shades of gray than black or white with eight stories exploring the nature of completions. He-Said / She-Said takes a turn in "It's Mutual". "Nor Did I" explores the power of the comeback when life has you down and people continue to pile on.

Endings happen to people of all ages, even those who have only begun to live. Duck-Young is an "Ageless Character" who shows that chivalry may not be dead after all, while a straight-A student does what it takes to maintain her GPA in "The Ends Justify the Means".

Endings can also entail monumental makeovers that don't lead to clean endings or beginnings. Things don't go as planned for a "Sorority Girl" who volunteers to help her sister, and Justine re-establishes herself once she commits to being "Gone" and finds the miracle in daily living.

While the results are the same, the endings are completely different for two characters. In "Silent Night" a man reconciles a missed opportunity to say goodbye. Meanwhile, Neil never sees it coming in a powerful manifestation of "Be Careful What You Wish For".

Beyond

What happens when what is beyond life as we know it touches a beginning, a middle, or an end? For better or worse may apply even on the other side. At "10:14" a random gift becomes a lifesaving good-luck charm. A glimpse into the future via "The Talking Board" may start a chain of events that Shannon would have been better to avoid.

Ever felt like there was a guardian angel nearby? A little "Roadside Assistance" and Officer Michaels in "Airborne" may make it easier to believe.

When you miss those who have gone before, there may be ways to prove that love never dies. Whether it's "Hugs" from Grandpa, "The Visitor" who is so familiar, or feathers from heaven that shout "I'm Here"…love's presence remains.

Ever wonder what happens on the other side? Find out about an unlikely "Reality TV Hell" that may change not only how you watch television but also how you view your life.

Moments - happy to tragic, temporary to permanent, cut-and-dry to ambiguous, and everything in between - make up a life. Now, it's time to explore the 24/7, universal phenomena that are *Life's Moments*.

BEGINNINGS

Awkward

Thomas waited for Olivia. The long day would be one he'd never forget. She was more beautiful than he could've imagined in the white dress. His heart stopped when he realized her eyes were locked on him as she walked down the aisle with her dad.

Her dad was the one who made his current situation more nerve wracking, thanks to his pact with his then teen-aged daughter, who was now Thomas's bride.

Thomas had his wild days, but that all changed when he walked into Paradiso Café and laid eyes on Olivia. She became his sole focus when she arrived at the table to take his order. The hint of an accent, her smile, her bronze skin, and those legs.

She hadn't gone without a fight. Olivia was her own woman with her own ambitions, but as Thomas found more excuses to visit the café, he found out that the willful woman also had an appealing traditional side too. In clichéd terms, he'd gotten to some of the bases but had never hit a home run. Now, they were aiming straight for a grand slam.

Olivia took a deep breath before opening the door. Her mind swam in thoughts of insecurity. *What if I'm no good? What if I do something wrong?* The questions continued. She smoothed out the shear, lacy baby doll nightie and told herself that she was beautiful, even if the thong was uncomfortable. *If things go according to plan it won't be an issue for long. You can do this. You've waited two years to do this. Heck, you've waited twenty-six years for this. It's time.*

She turned the knob without realizing she was holding her breath. The air escaped when she locked eyes with Thomas. He sat up. The collar of his tuxedo shirt opened wide. Sleeves rolled up. The pants inched up exposing his black socks. Somehow even his socks looked sexy. She returned to his eyes. They were dark, and he looked tense.

Disappointed? She thought.

Olivia misread the lust.

When the door opened, Olivia stood in the doorway in white, yet again, but his time it was a tease of white against her bronze skin. Thomas took in the white mesh and lace and immediately caught his breath. He zeroed in the shiny bow camped between her two gorgeous breasts. His eye trailed down to the sliver of a triangle peeking through the mesh just above the lace outline of the teasing piece of lingerie.

Neither said a word.

Thomas walked to Olivia and raked his fingers through her think black hair. Just before he lost more control, he stopped inches from her mouth.

"You're amazing."

The raspy voice silenced by a hungry kiss.

Olivia melted instantly. Her doubts disappeared. The feel of the lace rubbing against her chest as it rubbed against Thomas took the worries from her body.

When Thomas's tongue drove deeper and his hand seized her rear end, she groaned. Warmth and a body buzz began at her core and slowly migrated throughout her body.

Without thinking, she pulled at his shirt. When it was free from its tuck, she began to unbutton it, giving each plastic circle its proper attention before the shirt hung open completely. She wanted the shirt off. She wanted to feel Thomas, all of him.

Olivia slid her hands up Thomas's torso and chest. When she got to his shoulders, she pushed at the shirt, and Thomas slid out of it. She pressed herself against him and kissed him hard.

Thomas worked to maintain control. He wanted to consume her but knew better, for the moment at least. He picked her up without breaking the connection between their mouths and guided her legs. As Olivia straddled him, Thomas moved them to the bed and placed Olivia down. He undid his belt and let the pants fall to the floor as she watched. A quick flick of the socks sent each flying somewhere in the room. He took a breath and lowered himself on the bed and over Olivia.

Two years of waiting raised his desire to a fever pitch. He teased at the lingerie she wore and taunted various places on her skin.

Olivia could feel how hard he was through the boxers and wanted all of him. She propped herself up and slid her hand under the elastic. Thomas inhaled sharply as her hand circled him. The fleeting moment of panic about not knowing what to do passed quickly as

Olivia realized the power her hand held. She rubbed, explored, and found the effect of her actions exciting.

Thomas tried to get some of his senses back, but Olivia had all of his thinking abilities in the palm of her hand. He reached out and started with her shoulder. The strap slid off exposing the first rosy peak. He had to have it. He had to have all of her.

Thomas wrapped her up and tossed Olivia to her back. He began devouring her. Soon there was nothing separating them, and pure desire took over. Thomas hungrily thrust in and chased release.

As his tunnel vision faded, he looked down into Olivia's brown eyes. She smiled, but he could tell there was something more. He studied her face as he continued to gain his composure.

Awkwardness settled in as Thomas realized that Olivia didn't have one.

Thomas smiled. "It gets better. I promise." He paused. "You just drove me crazy. The first time's..."

"It's okay." Olivia interrupted with a smile. "I'm good. I was good."

"Good," Thomas sounded a bit defeated. "It'll be good at first, but wait until we figure out what really trips your trigger. Then it's bonus rounds."

They both smiled.

Olivia combed her fingers through Thomas's damp hair. "I'm sure it will be."

"You know the best part?" Thomas asked.

"What's that?"

"We have the rest of our lives to figure it out."

Career Day

It was the first race of the year: the first race that Beau wasn't sporting the yellow stripe on his back bumper. He was no longer a rookie, but the veterans still didn't completely trust the kid in close and fast quarters.

The biggest race of the year was winding down. His teammate and one of the biggest names in stock car racing was on his back bumper. The roles were supposed to be reversed, but the late restart put the veteran behind the newbie.

Later, when he watched the replay, he'd learn how much camera time he was getting. More importantly, he'd see how much his sponsors were getting. That was nearly as important as winning the race itself. It kept his butt in his ride. Things were dicey with sponsors after his resume of rookie mistakes left him with a reputation tied to wreckers rather than checkers.

Three laps to go, and Beau focused on what he loved, going fast and going to the front. Beau led his teammate and twenty other cars in the outside lane at the sport's most famous track. He didn't notice the fans on their feet as he whizzed by at around 200 mph. He did notice how the inside line pulled ahead though.

Along the backstretch, the two lines pulled even. Seconds before his mark into turn three, he edged ahead. The momentum carried through until the last third of turn four, and the inside line sailed passed. The red car to his left was replaced with a yellow one, and Beau dug harder.

Coming back to the line, Beau dipped lower on the track, testing. He did it automatically. He didn't have to think about it. It was going to come down to the last lap, last turn. The air and side draft buffeted the car at first. Then, it propelled it forward.

He stayed high in one and two to keep the speed up as much as possible for the backstretch. The car to his left slid up the track toward him. The other driver caught the car before they made contact, but it gave Beau and his line the edge. The outside line sailed forward while the inside line dropped six car-lengths.

Those behind his teammate were anxious and saw the opening. Coming out of turn four, the cars running third and fourth dove down to the inside and ran out in front of Beau's car. Beau and the outside line were three cars back when the white flag waved.

He could taste it. Then his mind started. *Was that a vibration?* Skipping the pits on the last yellow was a gamble. His tires were older than those around him.

"Fuel should be good." His spotter stated.

"Got a vibration," he stated, keying the mic as they exited turn two. His foot was still on the floor.

"Just drive," his crew chief responded. "Won't matter in a minute."

The lines were nearly side-by-side. The blue car leading on the inside was about a half car length ahead. His teammate stayed tucked behind him. Beau committed and drove the middle line to maintain speed while also trying to get some of side force to propel him. His teammate followed suit.

Halfway through turn four the lines were even. Beau willed more speed into the roaring engine. Blue was to his left. Coming out of the turn the car wanted to swing out to the wall, but Beau held it down.

"Inside! Inside!" His spotter's voice shouted.

A tire blew on the car behind the blue one. Beau didn't see the pile up of cars behind him. Beau focused on the line. He straightened out the final push as much as possible, even with the blue car on the inside. The blue car slid right. They touched. It was just enough to break Beau's run.

The blue car sailed to take the checkers with Beau hundredths of seconds behind.

Beau pulled his car down pit road and glanced at the smoke from the burn out under the flag stand. He felt like he could chew through his straps and helmet too. "So damn close," he muttered as he pulled his helmet off and tossed it to the right.

He climbed out and slipped on his sponsor's cap. A bottle was shoved in his hand as a reporter with a mic and a cameraman in tow stopped beside him. It was his first after race interview. It was nothing. He wanted to be in Victory Lane instead.

"What a finish!" The reporter smiled.

"Yeah, it would be better if it ended in Victory Lane though," Beau stated as his took a drink from the bottle and toweled his face off.

"Do you think older tires cost you the win?"

"Dunno. Maybe. Maybe not."

"Do you think the wreck cost you the chance? The 93 could've pushed you for the win."

"Maybe. I didn't see what happened. I was focused getting to the flag."

"Second may not be what you hoped for, but it looks like a great start to your second season."

"Yeah, I guess. Still it could have been better." Beau took another chug and remembered to do the sponsor routine before the reporter chased down the other top five finishers.

The crew pushed the car towards post-race inspection as his crew chief pulled him aside. "Listen. It's not Victory Lane, but you did have a career day. It's your best finish so far and pays serious bank."

"I guess."

"I've been around long enough to know," the older man leaned in. "Anyone who could do that here with a wheel going down has a bright future."

"What do ya mean?"

"Look," the man pointed to the car that was turning towards the garage. "Your tire was going down like you thought. Still, you brought it home for second. You got skills, and you've also got what's most important."

"What's that?"

"Luck."

Baby Steps

Faye freshened up in the restroom at the end of her work day. She was relieved that her boss had meetings all afternoon, so her distractedness wasn't noticed. *What am I doing?* She thought as she stared at herself in the mirror. *You're 54. You haven't done this in 20 years.*

The door swung open, and Gale breezed in. "Getting ready for your big date?" The fellow secretary asked.

"This is stupid," Faye muttered.

"What's stupid?" Gale stood beside her but talked to her through the mirror. "A date? Who are you kidding? You're a sexy lady. You've got needs too. Why not?"

"It's been 20 years, and that was with a body 20 years younger too."

"Hold on. You've still got it. It's not like you're jumping straight into bed. You're looking for companionship. Nothing wrong with that. Think of it like shoe shopping. You're just trying on a new pair. You don't have to buy them."

"Yeah right. I'm supposed to forget that my husband tried on a new pair and threw the old one away?"

"Ex! Ex-husband, and he's nothing but an a-hole. You're not *old*. He's just stupid."

Faye rolled her eyes. "How am I supposed to do this?"

"Stop it already. Relax. Don't make it bigger than it is. You're meeting a man that you have known for months. You're just spinning out because he asked you out for an official date. You're not curing cancer or going on a suicide mission. It's just a date" Gale fluffed her hair.

"What if he doesn't like me after tonight?"

"I doubt it. Come on. He's already shown an interest. Give yourself a break. Think of it as a date with Mr. Right Now rather than Mr. Forever." Gale turned to look Faye in the eye. "You're not going to get married. You're going on a date."

Faye nodded at nothing in particular.

"Where are you going?"

Faye took a deep breath. "Dinner at King's Ranch Steakhouse." She began running lipstick over her lips and blotted it on a towel.

"Good. Be sure to start with a big glass of wine. That'll take the edge off and get things going," Gale winked and peered into Faye's purse. "Do you have condoms?"

"What! Gale, good Lord!" Faye shouted.

"What?" Gale said innocently. "It's not like you're a clueless virgin. You were married for 20 years and have two kids that can make babies of their own. A lot's changed in 20 years. Girls are packing now. Gotta be protected, you know."

"I'm not jumping into bed with him. You said it yourself. Anyway, Mother Nature took care of that a few years ago."

"I'm not talking babies. You know that nursing homes have some of the highest incidence of STDs," Gale stated matter-of-factly.

"Geez, thanks. Now you're talking about nursing home folks while discussing my date," Faye shifted in her heels. It was the first time in a year that she had worn heels, and they were already killing her feet.

"I'm just saying. If you see him popping a blue pill, you'll be happy I mentioned it."

"There'll be no blue pills or anything like that tonight," Faye stated curtly.

"Girl, don't get your panties in a bundle. *Reeelaaax*," Gale emphasized. "While you're at it use more of what God gave you."

"What?" Faye stopped putting her make up back in her bag.

"You're girls are still fabulous. Show 'em off," Gale pointed to Faye's shirt.

Faye scuffed. Then, she studied her outfit in the mirror. She slipped off the jacket, unbuttoned another button on her silk shirt. Then, she adjusted the girls a bit.

"Work it, girl! Work it!" Gale shouted as she entered one of the stalls.

Faye chuckled and gave herself a final once over.

Gale's disembodied voice added, "Knock 'em dead, and don't forget...I want all the juicy details tomorrow."

Faye laughed, stood tall, and replied, "Here goes nothing."

"Nothing…Something…Just go have some fun."

A Model Discovery

Terri loved walking the bookstore. She was a book nerd, just like her parents. At twenty-four, the college student should be on a date at eight on a Friday night, but she happily wandered the aisles once her parents split to pursue their own interests.

There were two floors to the store, so after a quick round on the ground floor, Terri headed for the stairs. As she approached the central staircase, Terri felt totally happy and at peace. She was happy in her skin, and the thought struck her as funny. Her body image wasn't exactly great, but it wasn't bad either, though an earlier battle with severe acne took a toll on her self-confidence.

Terri decided to play up the random thoughts. As she went up the stairs she pretended to be in a grand ballroom where all eyes were on her. There was a little extra sway in her hips, and it made her smile.

Keeping in line with the game, she paused at the landing between the two sets of stairs and looked out over the ground floor. There were no gowns or tuxedoes. People were scattered among the shelves with their heads in books. The ones that weren't scanning pages were walking around or were in the process of checking out. Her inner diva wanted to wave to the inattentive masses as part of the charade.

The practical Terri, instead turned, and continued up the second flight. Still, she walked like she was royalty, even if it was only as a bookstore princess. After getting lost in the books upstairs, Terri made her way back down to find her parents. Her illusions of being the belle of the ball were forgotten. The stairs were simply a means to an end. She was on a reconnaissance mission to locate her parents.

"Excuse me," a man's voice said, but Terri didn't register that it was for her. "Um, excuse me, miss."

Terri stopped as an older man in a suit approached her.

"I noticed you walking up and down the stairs. You have a presence, you know." The man began. Terri remained polite though she stopped listening. *What a cheesy line.* She thought as she looked over the man with gray hair, Santa Claus belly, and a suit that had seen better days. *Man, he could be my grandpa. I always seem to get the whack jobs.*

The man handed her a card, and Terri snapped back into the moment. "I'm a modeling agent. I couldn't help but notice you. You have that "it" thing. I'd love to have you come to the office to talk." He smiled. He didn't look like a letch, so she took the card to be nice.

Model? Yeah right. Five three and curvy is not model material. She thought with her pleasant poker face.

"How old are you?" The man asked.

"Twenty-four." Terri knew that was a test. She was not jail bait, if he was a freak or predator. She was also well past the right age to launch a modeling career. Living in L.A. she knew a little about the realities and craziness of that world. Models are put out to pasture as thirty approaches. She was born and raised in L.A. with no aspirations for acting or modeling, but she'd watched dozens chase the dream.

The man frowned. Terri wanted to laugh. It may have been because she was actually of age, but her hunch was that it was because he now saw her as long in the tooth.

"Well, I'd still like to see you in my office," the man stated. "Call me and make an appointment."

"I'll do that," Terri smiled as the man quickly retreated.

She found her dad, and told him what happened with the old man. Though she didn't take any of it seriously, she was smiling at the ego boost. Terri figured he was a guy with a little office in the Valley or Westside who never had a huge client. Still, it felt good. Her little act on the stairs actually did have an audience, and it made her laugh.

Her dad looked at the business card and heard her chuckle. He frowned as they locked eyes. "I don't like it."

Terri realized her dad thought she was still young and dumb enough to believe it all. It stung, and the smile faded. "Come on dad. It's just fun." She smiled again, and reached for the card.

He reluctantly handed it back to her as her mom walked up. The Sergeant in her dad stood there surveying the store as Terri informed her mom about the developments. Terri tried to keep everything light.

Her mom took the card. "He gave you this?" Her mom's voice and expression turned from one of simple interest to an odd sense of awe.

"Yeah," Terri looked at her mom as her expression changed.

"Adrian Meyer?" Her mom looked at Terri like she was seeing someone else.

"Yeah, I guess." Terri leaned over the card to read the name. She hadn't paid attention to it. "That's what it says," Terri chirped.

"He's...he's the one that discovered Shyla Taylor, the super model." Terri's mom continued to look at Terri like this was the biggest news ever. "I went to school with her. He discovered her while she was walking home one day."

"Cool," Terri shrugged, took the card back, and gave her dad a look.

Terri never called the man or set up an appointment. She kept the card on her dresser for years though. It always brought her a smile to know the man who discovered one of the first super models said that she had "it".

Adoption Day

There was a worn out feeling in the house. Jesse felt it for weeks. Something needed to breathe life into the place. By mid-morning on Sunday, Jesse knew what that something was.

He invited his little brother out on a drive. When they got to the gas station, Jesse picked up a newspaper, and threw it in the car as he pumped.

"What's this for?" His little brother asked as Jesse slid behind the wheel.

"Getting a dog." Jesse stated matter-of-factly.

"Does mom know?"

"Nope." Out of the corner of his eye, Jesse could see his little brother looking at him. "Not even sure there's one in there to get, so it's better to just explain it later."

They stopped for a burger and sat in the car while they ate and flipped through the classifieds. Jesse wanted a Lab, a yellow Lab, to be specific. Two columns of pet ads yielded three possibilities, but each listing noted a cost of $100 to $500 each.

Jesse refined his search with a simple statement. "I want a free dog."

He scanned the pages again looking for free offers. Six used the keyword. Two ads had phone numbers or addresses that were too far away to consider. Two more listed dog breeds that didn't interest him. He wanted a real dog, not a girly dog. That left two. One listed a husky mix. The other was a German Shepherd and Mountain Dog mix. Jesse had no idea what a Mountain Dog was.

Jesse read the ad to his little brother. "I guess Mountain Dog is code for found in the mountains," he said with a shrug.

"I dunno," his little brother offered between fists of fries.

"I'm gonna call," Jesse resolved.

An hour later and fifteen miles from home, Jesse knocked on the door of the house matching the address the lady gave him. The lady seemed to be in a hurry and was a bit gruff. "You can come in. We were about to take the remaining ones to the pound when you called." She walked back into the house without looking back to see if Jesse followed.

Jesse stood looking around awkwardly. There wasn't a single dog to be had, and he frowned.

"I figured it would be easier if we brought them out once you were here. They're in the back." The woman was talking and walking further into the house. "I'll let them in." Her voice became more of a shout as she got further away. "The mom might be a challenge, but we'll see if she warms up to you. I'll put her back outside if she doesn't."

"Okay," Jesse replied, though he doubted she heard him.

Three puppies bounded into the living room, and Jesse smiled immediately as they fell over each other. He dropped to the floor and welcomed the furry bundles of energy. The mom, a German Shepherd, walked in, surveyed Jesse, and quickly circled to lounge at the other end of the room.

Jesse leaned back against the chair that he sat in front of as the pups ran over to check in with mom. They returned to investigate Jesse.

"There's four left. The girls went quick." The woman stated as she sat down on the couch. "Only one of them left." She pointed to a tri color bundle in the middle of the puppy wrestling match. "That one."

"We need some peace around here, so the remaining ones are going to the pound. I'm tired of dealing with them. They were a surprise after Roxy here got loose a while back."

Jesse let the pups circle around and sniff him. He smiled as he watched. "I guess I should probably take the girl since we have a girl dog at home already. We've never had a boy dog before." Plus, he figured a girl wouldn't make his parents veto the whole thing outright.

The woman talked some more, and Jesse's eyes stayed glued to the three siblings playing wildly. He thought about his little brother still sitting in the car who refused to come in. Jesse knew the radio wouldn't keep him entertained forever, but the woman continued to talk.

A bundle of brown fur appeared to Jesse's right. Jesse didn't see the pup walk in with the others. He reached out to offer his hand for sniffing, and the puppy growled. Jesse pulled his hand back.

"Don't mind that one. He has an attitude. He doesn't like anyone." The annoyed woman dismissed the pup as it went behind the chair that Jesse leaned against.

Twenty minutes later, Jesse figured it was time to decide. None of the pups had really latched on to him. They were more interested in each other. "Well, I guess it's gonna be the girl."

The woman pursed her lips as if to say 'of course'.

Jesse ignored the look and reached to bring the girl pup to his lap. "We do have another dog that's older but a good girl. We have a big yard, and I go to the beach all the time." Jesse didn't know why he went into a sales pitch about his dog-owning background. "I'm looking for a dog that likes to take road trips."

He was petting the girl pup in his lap when a bundle of fur came around the side of the chair. The brown puppy never hesitated. He walked right to Jesse, pushed his sister out of Jesse's lap, plopped down in her place, turned to give Jesse a single lick, and sat as if to say "Okay, I'm yours."

The woman's jaw dropped, and Jesse laughed. "Well," Jesse smiled and petted the brown puppy. "I guess he liked what he heard."

Jesse watched the puppy melt into his lap. "It looks like *HE'S* adopted *ME*."

Home

Christine put the key in the lock and turned the knob. The walls were white, nothing in the rooms or on the walls. Still, she knew this would be home. The first home she would know since graduating college and marrying him. It took six months to get everything in order.

The scene replayed in her head. She rushed home from work that night to make sure dinner was on the table as he required, promptly at 6:30. Leaving work in time to catch the right bus was always stressful since he sold her car. The shopping and cooking to have dinner on the table when he walked through the door left her exhausted after a busy day at work. He opened the door at 6:15. "What's that?" He barked.

"Dinner."

"Looks like dog food." He walked over to a plate and poked at the chicken. "I want a steak. I bust my butt to provide for us and you can't make a real meal?"

She looked at the chicken sitting next to asparagus and rice.

"You're cooking for a man, your husband, not a chick. If you can't fulfill your obligations as a wife, you

29

shouldn't be working. You should stay home to do things right. Tomorrow, you'll…"

"Sorry." She interrupted before realizing the mistake.

It started with a raised hand. It ended with a broken arm along with other injuries. It wasn't the first time it happened, but she vowed it would be the last. It wasn't, but she put her plan into action. She did whatever it took to collect money and get away.

"Stop it." Christine shook her head to stop that line of thinking. "It's a new life and a fresh start. Leave it there."

Christine walked through the small apartment and out to the balcony, breathing in the fresh cut grass below and looking at the trees. Everything was so green compared to Arizona. "Green and fresh, indeed."

Christine grabbed her keys from the kitchen counter and returned to her car. It was the first step in her escape. It wasn't great, but it got her across seven states. Everything that was hers sat in the old Jeep Cherokee. Two hours was all that she had to pack before he checked up on her at work. Her co-worker's call gave her just enough warning to get out before he pulled up to the house.

Three trips up and down the stairs, and it was all inside. There wasn't even a place to sit. After driving for the last 24 hours, she wanted nothing more than to eat and to sleep. *Sleep would be good.* She smiled. Though tired, she knew what she had to do.

Fifteen minutes later, she was at the mattress store. Christine picked out the mattress that she wanted, not the hard-as-a-rock type that her husband had insisted on having. It was a comfy and soft pillow top. She stopped on the way back to the apartment and got bedding, bathroom supplies, and enough for the kitchen

30

to make some dinner and breakfast. Two hours later, she was waiting for her delivery.

The next morning she awoke after the best sleep she'd had in six years. She stretched, smiled, and went to make some coffee. It was time to get her plan together. The bed had been the first priority. Today would be a couch and getting a start on changing the bare white walls into something that felt like home. The coffee went quick. She hung the shower curtain and finished her morning routine.

It was a gorgeous spring day, and Christine breathed in the air fully and smiled at the sun. The day flew by with visits to stores of all types. She thought the shopping bug had died in her, but she quickly found the fun in completely reinventing her life. She got lucky when the cable guy was already at the apartment complex and agreed to hook up the TV as soon as she got it in the door. The couch arrived as she was making dinner. She sat down to spaghetti, wine, television and enjoyed the peace.

After dinner, she began to put together some of the furniture that she found throughout the day. The wine continued to flow as she read the sometimes questionable assembly instructions and figured out what to do. At the end of her first full day of freedom, she had put together five pieces of furniture. Christine scanned the apartment and smiled. The walls were still bare, with the painting supplies in the corner of the room, but it was starting to feel like someone really lived there.

It took a month of painting, hanging, and general tinkering to get to the point where Christine could say she was done. She did it all herself and loved every minute of it. Some days were challenging once she found her new job, but it all had been a joy to do. Every time she had an idea and ran out to get something that she envisioned, it seemed the exact item was waiting at whatever store she went to, like it was meant to be. The seemingly impossible had becoming surprisingly possible and even fun.

She stood in the middle of her apartment and looked around with a smile. Sure, there were still things to do to be completely free, but now, in this moment, she soaked it all in. *I did it!* Christine realized that in process of making it her home - all hers - she had found herself again.

"Thank you." She looked up to the ceiling. "For a while there, I thought you forgot about me."

Bucket List

Calen started it when he was ten. The "Bucket List" concept didn't exist at the time. It was simply a list of things to see and do in his life. He never wrote down, but it was real, if only in his head.

The first thing on the list was Pompeii. That story was the only one he remembered in all the years of elementary school readers. Something about the city frozen in time and the people stopped in their tracks called to him.

At 28, he was finally hitting some of those goals. After months of chemo, he resigned from the job that he'd worked so hard to get. About the same time as his boss was reading the letter, Calen boarded his flight to Paris. Cheap airfare made Paris the starting point and finale to the Grand Tour he'd wanted to take. He had three weeks, but he'd make it count like three months.

Calen walked off the plane and proceeded through customs. He found the train station and figured out the scheduling. First stop, Bruges, the Venice of the North. The real Venice would come a week later.

"I can get you on an earlier train to Brussels." The lady behind the desk explained.

"I'm good with the TGV. I'll wait the two hours." He smiled.

The woman shrugged.

"Just spent the night on a plane and could use some food and feeling like I'm not in motion for a while." He didn't want to admit that the last treatment still was dragging him down a bit. It was only a week ago, but the worst had passed already.

The contrast couldn't have been greater. The calm of the Paris station and high speed train to Belgium was immediately and abruptly replaced by the bustling crowd and hustle of the train station in Brussels at evening rush hour on a Friday. Calen winged it and only had to double-back once to find the train out to Bruges. In about an hour, he'd be at his official first stop.

As the commuter train traveled the Belgian countryside, Calen watched the scenery. The sun was low in the sky and a haze hinted that it would be a foggy night closer to the coast. Now that he saw it firsthand, Calen understood the lighting and mood of many of the Dutch masters he'd studied. The feeling of being a kid at Christmas rose in him. *The adventure begins!* He thought.

The train lurched to a stop at the station. As he stepped onto the platform, reality set in. He had a backpack, rail pass, passport, wallet, and a general idea of what and where he wanted to do and see. That was it.

The sun set while Calen got his bearings. He didn't have a map and simply let his feet guide him. The need to find a place to stay was mediated by the slightly surreal feeling of walking the cobblestone streets and looking at the shadows of the old buildings.

Walking for more than an hour, with no overall sense of things, started to drain him. The first hotel option looked well out of his price point. Luckily, he found a small shop and stopped to buy a couple of beers for later. He wasn't sure where he'd actually be drinking them yet though. He noticed the door of another hotel and gave it a shot, thinking he was on the outskirts of the town by now.

"How many?" The woman behind the desk asked skeptically.

"One. Just me."

"We do have one room left." The woman began. "It's small and at the very top."

"Not a problem," Calen smiled. "Just need a shower and a bed."

"It has that." The woman smiled, and Calen grinned when he found out the room was budget-friendly.

The woman showed him to the room. She wasn't kidding when she said it was at the top. The three steep flights of stairs would have been better described as ladders. Calen's tired body wanted to rebel, though his mind kept it in check.

The woman opened the door, and he looked around. It was comfortably budget with a step up shower. "I'll take it."

"I'll need your passport." She put out her hand. "We'll take care of everything in the morning. Breakfast is downstairs."

"Great." Calen grabbed his passport and handed it over. "Thanks."

The woman nodded and quietly closed the door.

Calen dropped his pack on the bed and made a shower the first order of business. Feeling more human afterwards, he grabbed a beer and opened the window. The window was just a touch higher than his eye line.

Clip, clop. Clip, clop. Clip, clop.

Intrigued, Calen hoisted himself to sit on the window sill. His right leg dangled inside the room. His left floated in the air, four stories above the cobblestones below.

Glancing down, he identified the source of the sound. A horse-drawn carriage carried a couple. He watched as it got to the end of the block and turned right, out of sight.

Dong.

Calen was startled out of his quiet moment. *Dong.* He looked around the dark buildings. *Dong.* By the last one, Calen recognized what was directly ahead, Sint-Salvator Cathedral.

Despite having no clue where he was going and having no official game plan, he found a room with one of the best views in Bruges. He smiled, drained his beer, jumped down, got the second bottle and returned.

For the next hour, he watched people strolling in the darkened street, carriages passing by, and listened once more to the voice of the cathedral marking time. It was the perfect start to his once-in-a-lifetime trip.

He took it all in before climbing into bed. "Can't wait to see what tomorrow brings." He stated before dropping into one of the deepest sleeps of his life.

Can You Believe It?

Author Note: This story is dedicated to Rebecca, my true soul sista; her daughter and my soul niece, Xochitl, who is quickly becoming a beautiful Little Lady; and the man that brings them both love and joy.

***

It was a 24 hour period filled with surprises, drama, and trauma, but it was so worth it. She lay back in the hospital bed with the bundle wrapped in a pink blanket. "Baby Girl, you couldn't wait, huh?" She asked the sleeping baby.

The crowd of family had taken a momentary leave, and she enjoyed the quiet. She sighed while looking at the tiny face. As much as her heart swelled holding the little person who she'd come to know and love without having seen her, she was tired. She was told already that it would take some extra time before the baby could come home. The baby was healthy but still premature. It was just an added precaution.

Women lie. We are closed for business! She thought. *There's no way you forget about that nastiness.* She shook her head. *It was worth it though. I'm a mom now.*

A large man hovered awkwardly at the door. He was unsure whether to come in or not.

"Dad!" The woman exclaimed as a wide smile spread across her face.

He returned the grin and walked to the side of the bed. "I wasn't sure if you wanted to see anyone right now."

"You're welcome anytime." She reached to take the man's hand. "Meet your granddaughter, Stella."

He looked at the pink bundle and then to the woman holding her. He was in awe. It was the second time in his life that he saw his one and only daughter as a woman, more amazing than he could have ever imagined. *My little girl has a baby girl of her own.* He thought as his eyes glistened with tears.

"You're a mom now," the man's voice cracked as a tear escaped. He looked into his daughter's big brown eyes.

She smiled. She knew he was thinking about her as a baby, his baby, and then as his little girl. She thought about being that little girl and now she was a mom. Her eyes got teary as well.

"Yeah. Can you believe it?" She smiled and swallowed to get the lump out of her throat and smiled. She patted her dad's hand. "And…you're a grandpa now," she stated breathily as emotions swelled.

Both continued to grin in silence and looked to the new little life, now peacefully hanging with her mom and grandpa.

It was a moment that neither father nor daughter would ever forget.

MIDDLES

Birthday Wish

It was a late June morning when the boy walked into the kitchen to the smell of waffles on the iron.

"Happy birthday!" The woman at the counter exclaimed before wrapping her little boy in a big hug. "So, what does my handsome six year-old want to do today? I took the day off."

The boy with the big blue eyes smiled. "I wanna play baseball...with dad."

It was a dagger to the woman's heart.

"Well, how about if we have some breakfast and go to the park? I can throw a ball with you." The woman smiled in consolation.

"Sure," the boy's shoulders slumped as he stared at the kitchen table.

Neither said anything more as the waffles finished cooking. The woman added some whipped cream and chocolate chips, hoping that it would help distract her son from his missing father.

"Here you go," the mother placed the plate in front of her son. "Wait a minute."

She turned to a drawer and pulled out candles and matches.

"It's never too early to get the party started." She smiled as she placed six candles along the edge of the waffle and lit them.

The boy watched through his glass of orange juice as his mom set his waffle ablaze.

"Okay, make a wish and blow them out."

"But what about birthday cake?" The boy asked.

"That'll come later. There's no rule against birthday wishes over waffles." The woman nodded towards the plate-sized campfire.

"I wish…"

"Nope." The woman cut in. "You can't tell anyone your wish, or it won't come true."

The boy looked at her.

They both knew what the wish would be. They wanted the same thing.

He took a big breath and blew out the candles. He smiled, and she returned it with a pat on his back.

That evening the two returned from a day at the park, a movie, and dinner with her parents. The house was dark. The woman looked around the porch, but nothing was there. *Crap!* She thought.

The boy looked with her. She told him that the presents from his grandma and grandpa were only part one of his birthday gifts. There were more coming in the mail.

He wanted to see a box at the door. Then, he'd know that dad remembered too.

Nothing.

Again, the boy's shoulders slumped, but he remained silent.

"I'm sorry honey. They were supposed to be here today." The woman felt horrible but worked to cheer the birthday boy up. "I know there's still at least one more inside. I got it for you last week." She smiled and noticed the boy was forcing a smile. "They'll be here tomorrow. I'm sure," she reassured.

The key turned in the lock, and the boy waited for her to flick the switch inside the door. He was staring at the ground. She was at a loss for words. "We still have birthday ca…"

She stopped mid-word.

Standing up from the couch was the man in the camo. He had two presents in his hands that dropped onto the couch as he rose, bent over, and stretched out his arms for them.

"Happy birthday little man!"

"Dad!" The boy screamed and launched into the man's arms. "You're here!"

"Yes, I am," the man in the uniform said. "I wouldn't miss it."

Tears came to the woman's eyes as she watched to the two men in her life embrace.

She had to stop herself from doing what her son did. Her husband motioned her over anyways, and she went without hesitation. She melted into his arms for the first time in more than a year.

"How long are you here for?" She asked when she finally found her words again.

"I'm not on leave." He smiled and kissed her. "I'm here for good."

The boy stepped away from his dad's side and looked at his mom. "Mom!"

"What?" The woman moved her head to look down at the boy.

"Birthday waffles work!"

Genie in a Bottle

NOTE: This story was first published by Janelle Jalbert in the *Flash Fiction* online magazine.

***

"Here's to failure," Maggie raised her glass of bubbly and clinked it to Steph's glass of Jack and diet.

"It's not a failure." Steph's nose wrinkled. "It's taken two years to get that P.O.S. out of your life."

"Yeah, but still."

"No 'but stills'. You've got a whole new life to look forward to. You're sexy and brilliant."

Maggie threw her head back along with the cool bubbles in the glass. "Hit me."

Steph smiled and filled Maggie's glass. "Here's to freedom," Steph said pointedly.

"Wish there was a genie in that bottle to fix my messed up life," Maggie muttered.

Three years earlier it had been Stephanie toasting the end of her marriage. Now, it was Maggie's turn.

"So, tomorrow," Steph began. "It's a girls' day. Mani, pedi, hair, new clothes, and a night on the town."

"Mmm. I'm…"

"Bull!" Steph shouted. "It's a done deal. Time to get back on the horse, cowgirl. You've been moping for months...though I don't know why. He's a POS. College intern...so cliché."

"Thanks for reminding me," Maggie stated flatly. "I was an intern when we got together."

"That was different. He was an intern then too, but he wasn't married." Steph got up for another drink. "Okay, okay. So, tonight we drink like fishes and get our game plan together. Tomorrow, we conquer the world."

By 4 o'clock the next day, the ladies had gotten over their hangovers and completed their makeovers. "We need drinks," Steph stated as they left the boutique, wearing their newest acquisitions.

"Do we really have to wear these now?" Maggie pulled on the fabric of the red dress. She rolled her eyes towards Steph. The lyrics to "Roxanne" played in Maggie's head in the bright summer afternoon sun.

"Damn straight. We're sexy as hell, and I'm not giving you the chance to crawl back into your rags. It's time to flaunt it, if you've got it."

Maggie opened her mouth.

Steph quickly added, "Oh honey. You got." Steph nodded at Maggie, who alternated between pulling her dress up to cover her chest and pulling it down again as the hem crept up higher on her thigh. Steph playfully swatted at Maggie's hand to stop the nervous tug of war.

The pair walked into happy hour. The place was packed. Still, a high top became available as Daniel motioned for the women in sit down.

"Here." He patted the seat that he held out for Maggie. "Whatcha drinking?" Daniel asked, as he kept his hand on the back of Maggie's seat.

Dumbfounded, Maggie replied, "Uh…Chardonnay I guess."

"I'll take a Jack and diet," Steph added with a smile.

Daniel went for the drinks. "See. You're already back in the game."

Maggie rolled her eyes. "Great. Nothing smacks of desperation more than a tight red dress in the middle of the afternoon. Surprised Daniel's here."

"Wow, what a surprise," Steph stated in the deadpanned voice of obviousness. "He's only owned the place since his dad died."

"Maggie," Daniel sat drinks down in front of the women. "I haven't seen you in a while." His smile faltered momentarily as his eyes made it down to the hemline that had inched up on Maggie's leg. "Hot date?"

Maggie inhaled. Stephanie put a hand to her chin as she watched.

"Uh, no not really," Maggie stated.

"We're celebrating Maggie's freedom," Stephanie interjected with a smile.

"Freedom?" Daniel asked.

Stephanie noticed the way Daniel unconsciously took a step closer to Maggie and returned his hand to the back of Maggie's chair. Stephanie wondered if this was something new. Was it like in college too? Maggie seemed to have gone mute and remained silent while looking at Daniel.

"Yeah, she finally ditched the bastard."

"Oh, you're not with Kirk anymore?" Daniel asked.

"No, it was official yesterday." Maggie found her voice. "It was over a couple of years ago though."

"Sorry about that," Daniel unlocked his eyes from Maggie's gaze and looked at the table. "You were always too good for him."

"Yeah right." Maggie stated and brought her glass to her lips.

Daniel shook his head. "Hold up. It's supposed to be a celebration, right?"

Maggie shrugged.

Daniel smiled and motioned for them to wait before going back behind the bar. The women shared a tightlipped smile, shrugged, and continued with their drinks.

Daniel returned ten minutes later with three large mugs. One had beer. "Okay, supersized Long Islands are in order for the ladies." He smiled.

The women groaned with a flashback to their college days. Whenever there was a breakup or other drama, their groups of friends, including Daniel, would solve it all or forget it all with Long Islands.

"What about the restaurant?" Maggie asked.

"Night manager's here now. Told him I had some VIPs to take care of," Daniel smiled and toasted with the women.

The next morning, the doorbell shot Maggie out of bed as part of a cruel joke. She looked around the bedroom with squinted eyes and a roar in her head. Her red dress was thrown to the floor. Other articles of clothing were strewn nearby. She turned. The bed was empty. Then, the doorbell blasted again. She pulled on her robe and looked through the peephole.

"Figured you'd need this." Daniel smiled from the other side of the door and held up a bottle.

Maggie opened the door.

He didn't notice her wild hair or the smeared remnants of her makeup. He laughed at her perplexed look though. "I told you when I dropped you off that I'd swing by to pick up your car this morning." He handed her the bottle. "Best cure for what ails you."

Maggie continued to stare and took the bottle without a word.

"Don't ask what's in it. I call it Genie in a Bottle."

Addiction

Cat was halfway through yet another shift at the frozen yogurt shop when the woman walked in, as usual. There wasn't a day Cat had seen the woman come in since she started the job three months ago. Cold or hot, weather didn't matter. The woman always got a quart of yogurt. Cat found out quickly that the woman had an obsession when she got schooled for air pockets in her hand-packed work.

"I'll take a quart of the peanut butter chocolate." The rail thin woman stated after a polite but tight smile.

"Okay," Cat said with the quart container already in hand.

Cat pulled the lever and watched the frozen snake of brown circle around inside the container. When it got to the top, Cat moved over to the counter and pounded the container on the counter. The frozen contents settled, and Cat returned to the dispenser to add more. Pounding again and then topping things off before the lid shoved everything down and into place. Cat knew the woman was watching every move.

"That's five seventy-five," Cat said as she placed the white container in front of the woman at the register.

The woman had her money ready.

Cat hit the button on the register and made the change. "Here you go," Cat handed over the bills and a silver coin. "You must be addicted," Cat laughed. "How do you stay so thin eating this every day?" Cat asked before thinking that maybe she should mind her own business. "I mean, I've worked here for a few months and have packed on almost ten pounds," Cat deflected.

"It helps things flow better," the woman said, focused on the container. The woman looked up and gave another tight lipped smile before turning and leaving.

That night the woman sat in her house. An empty donut box mocked her from the floor. Candy bar wrappers dotted the coffee table. Deflated potato chip bags and empty jars of ranch dressing mocked her. She looked to her right, the white quart-sized container held only the residue of Cat's work, with a spoon sticking out of it like a flag. The guilt combined with the bloat gnawed at her gut.

It was time.

She got up and went to the bathroom to do her before-bed ritual. The woman closed the door, though she lived alone, and dropped to her knees. Minutes later, she wiped her mouth, brushed her teeth, washed her face, and weighed herself for the third time that day.

The bloat was gone, but the guilt remained.

Quota

"Okay, class. Since this is the first day back after Christmas, we're going to talk about starting the year right." Mrs. Kearney addressed the class of thirty squirming fifth graders at Sunnyside Church School. "We're also going to help Wendy prepare for her family's missionary trip."

Nearly every head turned to the blond haired girl in the back corner.

"As you know, Wendy and her family are leaving soon. They will be gone two years. They are going to Africa to help people come to know Jesus." Mrs. Kearny continued to talk, but Nina stopped listening.

Nina thought about being gone two years. It seemed like forever. She didn't think that she could do it, but there was no way her family would do something like that anyway. They couldn't take trips. Her mom needed to see her doctors every month.

Mrs. Kearny's voice brought Nina's thoughts back to class, as the teacher hovered over her. "For part of our Bible study today, I have asked Wendy's dad to come in and talk about the trip they're taking. This is Mr. Bolton."

Wendy's dad stood up from Mrs. Kearney's desk and began talking. Nina drifted off into her own thoughts again as the man spoke.

Nina had to go to the bathroom and looked around the room for Mrs. Kearney. She was standing at the open back door. *She's not even listening to Wendy's dad.* Nina thought. It added to Nina's dislike for the teacher. Mrs. Kearney talked funny, said weird things, talked about some place called Oklahoma all the time, and was just mean.

Since Mrs. Kearney wouldn't see her hand up in the air, Nina went and stood behind her teacher, waiting to be seen. Mrs. Kearney talked with Miss Pate, the teacher from the next room. They talked about different people and some students.

Nina shifted from foot to foot as she waited.

"I know Nina has a hard life at home," Mrs. Kearney stated. "You can't help but wonder if it's a test or some sort of punishment."

Nina froze.

"That's a bit harsh. Don't you think?" Miss Pate replied.

Nina stopped listening. She didn't hear what her teacher said. *Punishment for what?* She thought.

"Oh Nina! Why are you standing there?" Mrs. Kearney looked at her with wide eyes.

There was silence.

Nina spoke. "I need to go to the bathroom."

Mrs. Kearney nodded and pointed towards the door down the hall before going inside. Miss Pate gave Nina a weird smile and returned to her class.

Nina didn't rush. She knew she wasn't missing anything. She'd heard tons about Wendy's family and was kind of tired of it. It seemed like they had talked about going away forever already. The pastor, principal, and adults who worked at the school talked about it. They had fundraisers, but Nina was told it was okay if her parents couldn't give anything because they understood. Whatever that meant. She never felt bad about her family until she got to Mrs. Kearney's class.

She knew that she couldn't stay away any longer, so she walked back to class. She slowed at each open door and wished she was in those classes instead. Finally, the dreaded door was in front of her. Nina went through it and quietly took her seat. Some kids were asking questions about the trip, and Nina tried to look interested in the answers. Mr. Bolton finished and thanked the class for being good.

"Now, like Mr. Bolton said, it's important to share the Good News with others. That's your job as a Christian," Mrs. Kearney began.

Nina felt tightness in her stomach. No one ever talked about being a Christian as a job. She'd been in the school for six years and didn't understand why Mrs. Kearney was the first to talk about that.

"Every year, I decide to save a certain number of souls. It's what you should do. It's what every good Christian must do."

The tight stomach turned to a burning one. *I'm not a good Christian since I don't save enough souls? God loves me. Isn't that enough?* Nina's stomach felt like fire, and she wanted to say something. She HAD to say something.

"Now we're going to decide how many souls each of us will work to save this year," Mrs. Kearney smiled.

Nina continued to fight her burning stomach.

"Fifty!" Luke shouted out.

Nina looked at him and rolled her eyes. He always was trying to get on Mrs. Kearney's good side.

"Good Luke, but let's be sure to raise our hands," Mrs. Kearney said in her weird voice.

Hands shot up. Mrs. Kearney looked around the room, deciding who to call on. She was just about to call on someone, when Nina raised her hand. Nina never raised her hand, so the teacher's eyes immediately shot over to her.

"Nina?" Mrs. Kearney looked pleased. "How many souls are you going to save this year?"

Nina took a breath. She knew what she was going to say and had a feeling there would be a problem. Still, it had to come out. She took a breath and let it go. "When did heaven get a quota?"

Mrs. Kearney's eye got wide and her mouth opened. The class was silent.

Mrs. Kearney blinked. Then she raised her hand and pointed to the door. "Go see Mr. Wilson." Her voice was deeper than it had ever been.

Troublemaker Erick laughed to Nina's left. He was the one who was usually sent out. He even bragged about breaking two of Mr. Wilson's paddles during his repeat visits. Nina looked at him and then to Mrs. Kearney before walking out the door without saying another word.

Five minutes later, Nina waited quietly outside the principal's office.

A Dollar Matters

2004

The mechanic was an old friend. He'd been fixing Darren's cars for years. The man in the dark blue uniform bent under the hood of the car as Darren watched from his home office.

Darren didn't want to hang up the phone an hour ago. He wanted to keep Steve on the line. As long as his son was on the phone, the plane wasn't taking him towards the front lines. Darren was proud of his son and his choice to become a Marine, but now Darren's stomach seized. Instead of picturing the twenty year-old man Steve was today, Darren only saw images of the young boy that grew up sleeping in the next room.

Two hours later, Darren had paced his office and the halls. He had stared at his computer unable to deal with any of his work. There was a knock on the backdoor, and Darren walked to the kitchen.

The familiar face smiled. "Hi Darren, she's all fixed and ready to go."

"Thanks." Darren stated flatly.

"I did the service. Replaced the rear brakes." The mechanic handed the work order to Darren.

"Uh, come in. I'll get you a check. You want something to drink?"

"I'm good. Thanks." The mechanic stated as he crossed the threshold.

"Okay then. Gimme a second." Darren went to his office and returned, writing the check while walking. "Thanks for the house call. I didn't want to miss the phone call to today."

"No problem." The mechanic tucked the check in his chest pocket. He looked at his customer, one of the long-timers that he considered a friend. "Everything okay?"

"Yeah," Darren stared that the floor. "It's just that Steve left for Iraq today."

"Marine, right?" The mechanic asked.

"Yeah, off to the desert."

"I was a Marine. Nam. Lost a good friend. It changes you. That's for sure." The mechanic smiled despite the tough topic. "You've gotta be proud, but at the same time you've gotta be worried like nobody's business, right? Where's Moira?"

"She went out with her friend. We're dealing with it the best we can. Steve's her baby, so I get it."

"You know what?" The mechanic waited for Darren to look at him again. "Think I'll take a drink, after all. If you don't mind. I don't have any more appointments scheduled this afternoon, so I think I can squeeze in a breather."

Darren stood taller. "Sure. What'd you like? Water? Soda? Beer?"

"Cold beer sounds good, but I'll only have one. That's my limit now."

"Cool." Darren pulled the bottles from the fridge and popped the tops before the two sat at the dining table overlooking the backyard. They talked about life and worked around talking about the events and worries of the day.

"Thanks for sitting with me," Darren said as the mechanic closed the door to his truck.

"Thanks for having me in." The truck roared to life. "Remember, anytime you're worried about Steve..." The mechanic nodded his head at Darren.

"I will, and thank you." Darren tapped his shirt pocket and then the bed of the pickup. He watched as the truck pulled down the drive, turning onto the street.

2014

Darren had never been to the mechanic's house, but his widow called about some of the items in the garage. He pulled his truck up to the modest house and backed into the drive to making loading things easier. The supplies were going to the community center to help with the auto repair training program.

An elderly woman met him at the gate and walked him into the garage. They made small talk as Darren pulled the items that he thought would benefit the program most.

"Thank you again, Tracy. This will help out a lot." Darren stated, unsure of what to say to the woman who looked lost in the packed garage.

"I knew you'd find a use for it. Eddie talked about all the good work you do for the community center. He'd want to help out." The woman smiled. "There's something else I found. I think it belongs to you. Come in and have a seat while I go get it."

Darren had no idea what she was talking about but followed her lead. She disappeared deeper into the house as his took a seat on the couch.

Minutes later she reappeared, and sat in the chair next to the couch. "I found this when I was going through his things. It was in his wallet. It had your name and your son's name on it, so I figured it belonged to you." She handed the paper over to Darren.

As he extended his hand, his stomach lurched. Darren looked at the torn dollar bill and the mechanic's messy notation:

Darren Woodhouse
Steve Woodhouse
3/15/2004

He took a deep breath to clear the knot in his throat and stood to pull his wallet out from his back pocket. Darren sat down again with the torn half of the dollar bill resting on his leg. Without a word, he pulled a similar piece of paper out of his wallet and put the two pieces together. They matched perfectly.

Darren smiled at the woman who was watching him. "Ed gave me this the day that Steve left for Iraq." He took a breath. "I was worried about him. About whether he'd come back safe." Darren paused again. "Ed sat with me that afternoon. Before he left, he pulled out a dollar bill and tore it in half. He handed me half and told me to look at it any time I worried about Steve being over there. That way, I'd know someone else was always thinking about us and praying too."

The woman sighed.

"Steve came home safe." Darren looked at the pieces again. "I can't believe he kept it."

"Once a Marine, always a Marine." The woman quoted with a smile.

Rabbit

Willow was two exits from her coffee stop in Oklahoma City when road construction forced all traffic off the highway and on to a dirt bypass. It was an hour before the coffee place opened, but she needed a caffeine fix desperately. She slid into the opening between two semis and crawled through the dirt in her rental car.

Back on the highway, Willow took the first opportunity to steer around the semi in front of her. She knew she cleared the 30 mph sign before she hit the accelerator. Still, the glimpse of the trooper on the shoulder as she passed to the left of the truck made her cringe. She knew she wasn't breaking any laws, but the blue lights flashes in the rearview anyway.

"What the...I didn't do anything wrong!" She shouted as she pulled onto the shoulder.

"License and registration." The trooper leaned into the window. If he was legal to drink, it was only by a matter of days.

She leaned over to the glove compartment. "It's a rental." She said as she added the rental agreement to the license in her hand.

"What's that?" The trooper pointed to the GPS in the upgraded rental. It was a new car with only 121 miles on it before she took it east.

"GPS," she smiled.

"Follow me," the trooper gestured towards the cruiser.

Willow slid into the passenger's seat of the cruiser. It was odd that the trooper didn't watch her get out of the car. Seemed like an occupational hazard in his line of work.

She knew the drill. He didn't say why she was pulled, but it was obvious once again. Driving While Cali. It happened in every rental car on the eastbound drive.

"Where you headed?" The trooper asked as he punched at the computer keyboard.

"North Carolina."

"For what?"

Willow knew the game but was still irked by the questions. She smiled. *Fishing, are we?* She thought. "My work. I spend time on the road. Sales. On my way to Charlotte for a meeting. Need to be there tomorrow afternoon."

"Oklahoma's a long way out." His eyes glued to the screen.

"Yeah, no surfing here either." She quipped.

A car went by with Baja California plates. She glared at it speeding by. *And I'm the one that he thinks he's gonna bust for drugs?*

"I was just trying to get to the a coffee stop. I need caffeine. There's a place over there. Isn't there?"

"You come through here a lot?" A thin smile developed.

Great. You mention surfing, so he thinks stoner. Now he's onto the fact that you drive through often.

He's lining you up for sure. Willow sighed. "Like I said, I do a lot of traveling for work."

She knew it was coming. The upside of it would be that she'd get her coffee since the shop would open before she got there.

"You mind if I search your car?"

Willow shrugged and smiled. "Go ahead. There's nothing in there."

The trooper started with the front. She watched her purse get scrutinized in real life and on the dashboard camera. He proceeded through the front in quick order.

All of the clothes on hangers in the back were pulled out and put on the hood. Willow cringed knowing that her clean clothes were lying on the hood of a car that had already traveled 1,000 miles. Her work bag was next, but she couldn't see him shuffling through it on the backseat.

He zeroed in on the back seat itself like a dog scenting its prey. His hand went to where the back lid met the upholstery. He tugged and began pulling. She couldn't make it out through the camera or the windshield. A stream of clear plastic followed as he continued to pull. With the inanimate snake slain and tossed back into the car, he went to the driver's side.

He popped the trunk and bent over to start investigating. Her suitcase was followed by the iron and the gallon of water beside it.

Willow sat back in the seat and watched everything through the dashboard camera. She was just waiting to get the biggest, baddest coffee she could buy.

He was on to her toiletries bag. Really, it was a duffel bag. When she did road trips, she didn't both with travel sizes, so she used the small duffel instead. It wasn't until the trooper pulled out the rolled up blue towel that bells went off.

Willow straightened up and tried to watch through the video monitor and windshield at the same time. *Are you sure you wanna do that?* She thought with a mischievous smile. She had forgotten all about it until the moment she saw the towel. *This is gonna be fun.*

The trooper unrolled the towel and uncovered what it held. His hand and the towel blocked the view of the long plastic device with its little bunny strategically placed so the movement of its ears and nose would send a woman over the edge.

The trooper stopped cold. His eyes locked on the tool in his hand. Willow didn't hear it, but she knew the baby-faced trooper gasped.

Willow wanted to burst out laughing right then and there. She knew better than to be caught busting up at the trooper's expense. She moved her mouth side to side to stretch out any smirk that might remain.

The trooper never looked back. He threw everything back in the car and returned to the cruiser.

"Here's your paperwork. Everything's good," he stated without making eye contact.

"So, that coffee shop is just over there, right?" Willow said innocently, enjoying the trooper's embarrassment.

"Yes. Yes, it is. Right next to the 24 hour drive-thru. You don't have to wait for it there. You can get back on your way quick."

"Thank you," Willow grinned. It was the smile she had been stifling. She opened the door.

The cruiser sped passed her before she even got to the door of the rental car.

Vacation Splash

It was the first family vacation for the Johnson's in seven years and the last one to include the matriarch of the family. They pulled together the funds to attend a wheelchair tennis tournament in Hawaii that the youngest daughter was playing in on her rise through the ranks. During the tournament's down day, the family packed into the minivan and headed across the island from the North Shore to the bustle of Honolulu. They sat in a noisy, popular restaurant ready to have their "splurge" meal of their weeklong stay.

Two sat on each side of the table with Christy, the youngest at the head of the table in her wheelchair. Mom and Dad faced the eldest daughter, Kim, and her grandmother with menus between them all.

"What are you having?" Grandma asked Kim.

Kim stiffened and looked at her dad who stifled a smile. The night before, Kim was asked the same question by her Grandma. Kim shook her head slightly at her dad. *I know better today.* She thought. Grandma ordered first the night before and decided to have the same thing Kim was having, a Chile Relleno. It was Kim's absolute favorite Mexican food. When it came time for Kim to order, the waiter stopped her cold.

"Sorry, she ordered the last one," he pointed to the gray-haired woman beside Kim.

Kim fought hard not to gasp or complain, even a little, though she knew Grandma didn't care whether she had the Chile Relleno or not. Grandma didn't look at her or say a word. Mom and Dad watched without offering suggestions. Kim frowned. She ended eating tacos instead.

As the family left the restaurant, Dad put his arm around Kim. "You have to admit it's pretty funny."

Kim rolled her eyes. "Yeah, right."

"No good deed goes unpunished," Dad whispered in her ear.

"No doubt."

Today, Kim was going to have the Roasted Island Chicken Pot Pie with curly fries. She opened her mouth and answered Grandma's question. "I'm having the Island Salad."

Dad knew. He smiled at the seventeen year-old and went back to his own decision making.

The waitress arrived at the table and greeted everyone, making it a point to look Christy in the eye as she took down drink orders.

Five minutes later, the waitress approached the table of five with a large platter full of ten glasses. Five waters, two iced teas, two diet sodas, and a lemonade. The waitress held the platter at chest height in front of her. Minutes earlier she'd made a point of recognizing the girl in the wheelchair at the end of the table. This time the waitress completely forgot she was there. The tray blocked her view.

The waitress was at full speed when her hip slammed into Christy's shoulder. In what seemed like slow motion, ten glasses of iced liquids proved the laws of physics. Things stay in motion until acted upon by another force. A cascade of fluid rained over the head of Christy and landed in Dad's lap. His shirt and pants were covered. His hands flew up in surprise.

"Oh my God!" The waitress shrieked.

There was a flurry of activity as napkins and apologies were tossed around like the drinks moments before. "Your meal's free sir," the waitress offered as she tried to figure out whether to help wipe his shirt off or not. "Drinks for everyone too."

"It's okay." Dad grabbed a dry napkin. "I'm okay." He rubbed at his dripping shirt. "It's hot outside anyway."

When the commotion settled, the waitress regained her composure and pulled out her ordering pad. "What can I get you?" She started with Dad who chose a burger as he finished getting situated. Mom ordered. Then Christy.

Next Grandma. "I'll take the Island Salad," she smiled and handed the menu over.

"And you?"

"I'll have the Roasted Island Chicken Pot Pie and curly fries," Kim smiled.

"That's my favorite," the waitress chimed.

"On second thought, I'll have that." Grandma interrupted.

"I'm sorry, ma'am, but she got the last one," the waitress looked at the elderly woman who wrinkled her nose.

"The salad's fine then," Grandma stated.

The waitress left after another round of apologies.

"I thought you were having a salad," Grandma said with a touch of annoyance.

"I was. Then I changed my mind," Kim smiled and looked at Dad.

He roared with laughter.

Love in the Time of Online Dating

NOTE: This story was first published by Janelle Jalbert in *Flash Fiction* online magazine.

***

He hit send and waited for a reply. Two minutes later, Tim had a date. They had exchanged emails, texts, and a call or two over the last two weeks, so he decided to pull the trigger.

"Ok, McGrath's is good." The text read. "May be a little late depending on work. I'll be in a blue shirt with a red necklace in case you're not sure."

The next evening, Tim walked into McGrath's at six. He found two open stools at the bar and ordered a beer.

Diane's day was a nightmare from the second she walked into the office. By the time four o'clock rolled around, she just wanted to escape. Two hours later, she walked into McGrath's for a drink, before going back to her empty apartment. There were two single seats left open at the bar. She assessed the lesser of two evils.

"Is this seat taken?" Diane asked the dark haired man.

"No," Tim replied. "I've been saving it for you."

What a line. Diane thought as she took the seat and smiled politely. She played with her ruby necklace while she decided on what to drink.

"Tim." The man held out his hand. *Man, she's better than her pics.* He thought as he studied her blue eyes and dark hair.

Diana rolled with it. "Nice to meet you." She shook his hand.

"What are you drinking?" Tim asked.

"I'm thinking a margarita."

Tim ordered a margarita and smiled.

"Thanks. It was a helluva day at work." Diane let her guard down a bit at the gesture.

"Yeah, it's nothing like San Diego."

"Ah, I went to school in San Diego. Miss it. Could use a good beach day." Diana smiled at the thought of her college days.

"I'm looking forward to my next beach run," Tim stated with a smile and a toast as Diane's drink arrived.

Diane loosened up after her first margarita and a trip down a memory lane filled with happier times.

Tim was amazed by the way things evolved. He never knew she surfed, and her stories brought back good times in California. The conversation went from there and lasted for more than an hour. As they changed topics and kept the talk flowing freely, Tim realized that he wanted to learn even more.

"Listen, I came for a drink or two, but you're really interesting. I'm starved. Wanna join me next door for some dinner?" Tim asked.

Why not? Diane looked Tim over and nodded. It would save her from figuring out her solo dinner back home anyway. Plus, Tim seemed to have it together. She'd have broken her rule about not getting numbers from a bar if he made the offer.

As the pair felt a buzz from the drinks they had, they both loosen up and began to joke around. Each of them thought the other had potential.

Tim waved off Diane's motion to cover her share of the bill.

"Thank you, but you didn't have to." Diane smiled.

"I want to," Tim said, as he finished signing the receipt.

"Ready?"

"Sure. Let's go," Diane said as she grabbed her purse.

Tim followed Diane through the lounge and to the door. He was mesmerized by the way her hips moved in the tight black skirt that she wore below her blue shirt. Her heels added to the look.

When Diane got to the door, she didn't hesitate to open it, though Tim attempted to get ahead of her. As he took control of the door, a woman walked up. Tim was busy watching Diane and didn't notice her. He simply made sure that the woman in jeans and a blue shirt cleared the door before letting it go.

"Thank you," the dark haired woman said to Tim.

That's when he noticed the red beaded necklace.

It was a fleeting moment that Tim recovered quickly from by dismissing it. He caught up with Diane in a matter of strides. Tim opened the door to the steakhouse.

"Thank you," Diane said as she locked her blue eyes on his.

Ten minutes later, Tim's phone vibrated, but he ignored it because his attention was on the woman in front of him. When the restaurant closed hours later, he walked Diane to her car and watched her drive off in her sports car. She didn't ask for his number, and he had forgotten about anything outside of the last few hours.

Tim reconsidered sending the woman a quick message. Instead, he checked his texts and found the unread one. "Sorry I was so late. Guess I missed you."

That's when he realized that the woman who had captured his interest and full attention wasn't Cynthia.

Tim shouted into the night air. Despite being a semi-regular at McGrath's, Tim had never seen the woman, who left in the sporty ride, before that night. He'd never see her again, no matter how much he wanted to know more of her.

He took a deep breath and looked at his phone. His finger slid across the screen. "Stayed as long as I could. Maybe next time."

Awakening

Carol woke up before the sun came up. She beat the alarm clock by a half hour. She took a deep breath and stretched before getting out of bed. Carol shuffled to the coffeemaker and took care of business.

The growing light and rose colored clouds caught her eye to the east. Carol poured a steaming mug and walked out to her patio. The tightness in her chest was gone. The deep breaths felt good. Carol sat and looked at the pine trees. Birds came to life in a chorus of chirps. The air was cool but the perfect temperature. Carol adjusted her robe and sipped her coffee. She kept the day's to-do list at bay and simply breathed. Carol's mind hadn't quite awakened anyway.

The light slowly grew brighter, mirroring her soul. Carol realized how much she missed feeling calm and just being in the moment. Two squirrels chased each other around the trunk of the nearest pine, and Carol watched. They ran clockwise then seemed to switch without notice and do counter-clockwise spins around the bark. Carol continued to drink her coffee.

The sun broke over the horizon and the rosy, diffused light became more direct. A breeze rustled through the trees, and Carol noticed that the flowers in the nearby pots had sprung to life again at some point. She hadn't noticed before. Carol pulled her legs into the large wooden chair and laid her head back. Wispy clouds floated overhead as a jet, high above, shot across the sky taking people off on an adventure or back home again. Home. She'd lived in her little place on Oak Tree Street for decades. Still, it was the first time in what seemed like forever that she was home finally.

Inhale.

Exhale.

The faint sound of traffic on the highway a couple of miles away got gradually louder. More cars passed by on the street in front of her house. Dog's barked in the distance. She could tell they were barks from those watching someone walk by, and they wanted to go walk too.

A butterfly floated by a few feet from her.

"Ahh," Carol exhaled as any trace of stress disappeared.

It felt like the world was vibrating. Anything was possible again. Her heart leapt with joy. Life opened up in that moment. There was total peace. *This should be the way it always is*. She thought. Carol took another breath and soaked it in.

It's Tuesday. The caffeine driven thought came out of nowhere.

Carol smiled sadly. She returned to the kitchen and dropped her mug in the sink before walking to the shower. The steam felt good, even as Carol tried to ignore the weight returning.

She tried to hang onto the light mood from earlier while standing in front of her closet. Her choices reflected her outlook in the moment. She set aside the black and white business suit and picked a flowing print dress instead. Even her shoes were different. Strappy heels replaced the practical slip-on flats. Still the heaviness continued to build on her shoulders. Carol looked at herself in the mirror and caught a glimpse of the clock out of the corner of her eye.

That did it.

She let out a low groan and dashed for the door. Forty-five minutes of bumper-to-bumper traffic ground away any sense of contentment in Carol. The mad rush of emergencies and office firefights hit her before she could put her purse down. Before she knew it, she is hip deep in meetings and paperwork.

The peace wouldn't return to Carol for another seven years. Ten days after her retirement to be precise, though she could have found it at any point in the 2,555 intervening days. She simply forgot to look for it.

Gorilla in Our Midst

The campground was half empty when the couple decided to walk over the dunes to the shore. A bank of tall bushes lay between the campsites and the dunes, separated by intermittent trails leading to the water's edge.

During the walk, they came across a group of ten young girls hiking, chattering, and chasing butterflies among their chaperones.

"We're on a father-daughter camping trip for the scout troop," one of the men replied to honeymooners' question.

Two hours later, the honeymooners returned from their time by the water. Once again the group of excited girls crossed their path near the bushes. The woman pointed to the left, and the man followed her finger with his gaze. They stopped and exchanged smiles. In a break in the greenery, a man dressed in a gorilla suit, head in hand, got into position fifty feet ahead of the line of girls. He put the large furry head over his own and crouched down.

The couple moved to the left for a better view of the show. They watched the father at the front of the line slowly drop back to join the other two at the end of the unruly line. Step by step the girls closed the distance. The first girl nearly walked by the figure hiding in the greenery.

"RRRROOOOARRRR!"

The gorilla man shouted as he grabbed the first girl. The girl screamed and flailed. The second girl stopped cold. Frozen in place. Mouth open. The second girl took off past her captured friend. "AHH!"

A chorus of shrieks filled the air as girls scattered.

A couple of girls turned around and ran back the way they came. They were caught by two chaperones in the rear. The third man was doubled over in laughter.

The girls in the middle scattered through the bushes.

The honeymooners erupted into laughs so hard that they cried.

One girl scurried by them at top speed.

"Hold up! You're okay." the woman shouted.

The girl continued for several strides before stopping and turning around. "What?" The frightened girl asked.

"I think the gorilla is one of your dads." The woman said to the girl who cautiously walked towards the couple.

"The what?"

"The gorilla."

"Is that what that was?" The girl asked.

"Yeah, we saw him get into place."

"OMG! I'm gonna get him!" The girl turned from fear to pre-pubescent vengeance. She took off after the offender.

Shrieks could be heard in various directions throughout the campground as the girls scattered like roaches in daylight and continued to scream.

Those who were at the various campsites stopped and watched the aftermath without understanding what started it. The fathers went to wrangle up the escapees and explain the prank to those who were alarmed by the panicked children fleeing some unknown horror.

A half hour later, one of the chaperones walked up to the couple seated at their picnic table, while the campfire got going. "Hey there, have you seen a girl around here? Blond hair, blue eyes."

"No, we haven't." The newly minted husband replied. "One's still MIA?"

"Yeah, my daughter," the father looked concerned even through his smile. "Wanted to give them a surprise. Didn't think they'd freak this much."

"She's around. It was classic though. Saw the whole thing. Priceless."

"It'll be all good when we get the last fugitive." The man smiled again.

"We'll keep an eye out," the woman stated as she started walking to the car to get the food prepped for the fire. "Which site are you at?"

"114."

"Cool."

The woman opened the side door to get to the ice chest, and a little girl popped out from under a blanket behind the driver's seat.

"AHHH!" The woman screamed.

The girl screamed back.

The two men dissolved into laughter.

"Found her!" The woman shouted as she helped the girl out of the car and walked her over to her dad.

The men worked to control their belly laughs.

"Didn't expect a two-fer with this one. Sorry for the heart attack." The dad said to the woman, as he put his arm around his daughter.

"No problem. You're lucky I'm a good sport." The woman rolled her eyes. "At least all are accounted for.

"Classic. Truly classic though." The younger man said through his chuckles.

"I better not see any furry critters tonight during any bathroom runs, or I'm coming straight to 114 to help the girls finish you guys off." The woman warned.

The girl laughed from under her dad's arm. "Good! Girl power!" She ran off to join the other girls at their campfire.

"Thanks again." The dad said as he walked in the same direction.

"Thanks for the entertainment!" The man seated at the table shouted at the retreating figure.

"Ugh." She said before taking a long drink.

"No, it's more like *AHHH!*" Her husband corrected by mimicking her cry.

"Very funny. I'll give you something to scream about."

"I sure hope so. After all, it is our honeymoon."

Lightning Fast

Marvin, in his stars and stripes uniform, listened to the anthem with his teammates. The flag slowly lifting towards the rafters.

It wasn't the way he imagined it.

Since his fifth birthday, when his dad gave Marvin his first ball, he had wanted to play basketball. Marvin perfected his game during any free time he had. His tireless dribbling and shooting led him to jump straight to the varsity team as a freshman in high school.

Junior year was set to be the year that the college scouts would start to take notice but the family was forced to move. Marvin stood out even more as a star athlete at his new school, which made getting a scholarship and making it into the NBA seem even more possible.

Senior year, he was the leading scorer in all of Indiana throughout the entire season. Then came that Sunday night. The storm was a warm one for that time of year and brought flooding and high winds. The small rental house wasn't in the best condition, so it wasn't a surprise when the dripping water in his mom's bedroom became a steady stream.

Marvin didn't think twice about fixing the tarp on the roof. He'd done it plenty of times through the summer and fall. In fact, he kept the ladder up along the side of the house to make the job quicker.

Marvin climbed the ladder, despite his mom's protests. Once on the roof, he pulled the blue plastic back over the section of leaky roof. The wind blew hard enough to rock Marvin while the tarp acted more like a sail. It took a few minutes to get it secured with the bricks that littered the roof for that reason.

Marvin stood up to take one last look at his work.

In the months and years that followed, he wondered about Mother Nature's cruel trick. Light moves faster than sound. If it was the other way around, he may have known what was coming.

As Marvin stood atop the roof in the storm, light and electricity bolted from the sky. There were no trees around. The highest point at that time was a six foot tall basketball player standing on top of his roof. Lightning struck Marvin, knocking him from the roof. He landed on the fence separating the backyard from the front. He was paralyzed instantly – alive – but unable to walk again.

The surgeries and therapy sessions went on for years. Bitterness was a constant taste in Marvin's mouth as he learned to deal with a life that had new limits. His dream of a basketball career was gone in a flash. With it, he gave up on college too.

His doctors recommended a rehab hospital. They had a program that the doctors thought Marvin would be interested in. The next Wednesday night, his mom drove him to a high school twenty miles away. He rolled his chair into the gym and was greeted by a group of eight others.

None of the pitiful looks. No questions about why he was in a chair.

The coach, one of only three in the gym not in a wheelchair, walked over. "Jeff." He held out his hand.

"Marvin."

"You play?" The coach eyed him.

"In high school," Marvin replied.

"Able-bodied?"

"Yeah."

"That'll make it a little easier for you." The coach studied the young man. "That chair's not set up for play. Let's start you with some ball handling. You can try your hand at that basket over there. It's standard height, so be prepared to have to chuck the ball harder to make it in."

"Okay." Marvin looked at the basket to his right.

Coach tossed him a ball. "We're going through warm ups. Running drills. When you're comfortable you can join in if you want."

Marvin nodded and wheeled over to the empty basket with the ball on his lap. When the practice game started, Marvin could only watch. He looked at the straight up and down wheels of his chair and wondered why their wheels angled. The players moved the ball almost like they didn't have to think about dribbling and pushing a chair at the same time. Then there were the crashes. Bodies flew out of chairs and no one, even the onlookers, thought anything of it. A person bounced out of a chair simply jumped back in, and the game resumed.

Marvin didn't join in that night.

Coach went over to him after the game. "Whatcha think?"

"Intense."

"We're here every Wednesday at six. Could use a guy your size along the base line. How tall are you?"

"Was six four," Marvin swallowed the bitterness.

"That chair's gotta go if you're gonna play." The coach sized him up. "Needs more camber."

"Camber?"

"Angle in the wheels. Makes you turn faster. Those front wheels have to go too. They need to be smaller."

"I'm lucky I got this one," Marvin grumbled. *Even this type of basketball isn't gonna happen.*

"Next Wednesday, can you meet me that the hospital before practice?" The coach asked. "Say three o'clock."

"I guess. I'll have to see if mom can get off work." Marvin felt ridiculous for needing his mom to drive him around at age 21.

"Where do you live?"

Coach showed up at his home the next day. Marvin was fitted for a sports chair at the hospital and was allowed to borrow it, no questions asked. It was the third turning point of his entire life.

In the next two years, Marvin never missed a practice. His therapy sessions changed to workouts, and he began playing games throughout the region. The region became the country, and by the time the basketball team for the Para Olympics was put together, Marvin was the first player named to the team.

There he sat among his team, representing his country, with a gold medal around his neck as the anthem filled the arena.

The Girl Code

Trisha woke up early thanks to the sun streaming through her open blinds. The night had been a crazy one. Too many drinks while hanging out with her friends Sylvie and Boyd. She knew it must have gone sideways because Boyd's car was still under her bedroom window, but he wasn't in bed. Parts of the night were still missing. She didn't remember going to bed or much from the hours before that. "Time traveled again," she muttered as she pulled her bedroom door open. Her coffee pot was her singular destination.

She walked through the living room and into the kitchen. It was her daughter's weekend with her dad, but she looked through the cracked bedroom door out of habit. Sylvie was passed out in the pink princess bed. No surprise there. If she had drank enough to forget, Sylvie most definitely did too.

Trisha didn't notice the extra lumps in the bed next to the blond. She made her coffee automatically and groggily made her way to the bathroom. With the flush of the toilet came a moment of clarity.

Trisha walked back to the doorway of her daughter's room and looked in again. This time there was no mistaking the tuft of short dark hair on the pillow beside Sylvie.

"Son of a bitch!" Trisha shouted out.

The two lumps in the bed shot up. Sylvie had a slightly confused look as she reached for the comforter to cover up once again. Boyd's look that went from clueless to guilty as charged. The blonde's expression went from sleepy to smug.

"Uh, we..." Boyd stammered.

"Don't want to hear it," Trisha put her hand up to stop him. "Both of you. Get out!"

The two got up, threw clothes on, and began to explain once they got to the kitchen.

Trisha just raised her hand for them to stop and shook her head. The only other sounds to follow were two cars starting and pulling out of the driveway. Trisha remained at the table, drinking her coffee, feeling the double blow to her ego.

When she finally stood up, Trisha immediately went to the princess bed, stripped it down, and threw the evidence in the washing machine. That's when she snapped. There was no one but the dog to hear the tirade.

After the initial wave passed, Trisha tried to talk some sense into herself about the situation but found it outrageous. Eventually, she picked up her phone.

"Hey, what's up?" her sister's voice answered on the third ring.

"I'm pissed."

"What now?"

"Sylvie slept with Boyd." Trisha stopped there in order to process how to say the rest.

"What!" Her sister exclaimed. "You and Boyd are still together, right?"

"Yeah, we were still seeing each other."

"Then what the..."

"Gets better. They did it in the princess bed last night."

"Hold up! She sleeps with your guy. Under your roof. In your daughter's bed?"

The facts were settling in for Trisha as much as for her sister.

"That's beyond low," her sister continued. "There are just some things you don't do. And you wonder why I have so few gal pals."

"Yeah," Trisha murmured. It sounded lame, but it was the best she could do.

"That's the ultimate betrayal. Guys are stupid. They'll take anything offered, but she knew better. That's the most basic of girl code, even for the biggest backstabbers out there." Her sister sounded ready to rip Sylvie's head off. She had never liked the blond. "I'd kick her butt to the curb. There's no redemption for that. She knows you and Boyd have been an item for years."

"Yeah, but we're still casual," Trisha countered.

"I know you two have seen other people during that time, but if you were so casual, you wouldn't sound like a kicked puppy right now."

Trisha stayed quiet.

"It doesn't matter. He was with you, and she still slept with him. It would be one thing if she asked first. To move in for the kill all stealth is something else. No respect. In your house and in your daughter's bed too. That's just skanky. I'd drop her like nobody's business. It's wrong."

Months later, Boyd was history, but Sylvie remained.

No Good Deed

It was the first week that Sharon was in Savannah. She moved for work and decided to get to know her neighbors when the weekend arrived.

When the sun went down, people emerged from their air conditioned apartments. Sharon opened a beer and walked out the landing. Two neighbors were leaning against the railing on the ground level, talking with two women. Another group of neighbors walked across the parking lot to join the impromptu gathering. Sharon took her spot along the railing and was joined by yet another guy from upstairs.

The two women downstairs chatted with everyone before leaving for their girls' night out.

"Remember, Sharon, potluck. My place tomorrow night for the game," the brunette shouted up as she turned to her car.

"I'll be there," Sharon replied and finished her first beer.

She turned to the guy next to her. Her neighbor from upstairs was named "The Metrosexual" by the men around the complex, and the women who had fallen prey to his moves called him "STD". Sharon laughed at the thought as she turned to her door for another cold one.

During the evening, the group of neighbors bounced from location to location throughout the complex as people joined and exited. Sharon relaxed into the experience and found the dramas of this little slice of the South hilarious.

The gathering began to break up around 11:00. One of the guys in the group wasn't a resident. Wrench, the name he introduced himself as, was the friend of her downstairs neighbor. His buddy had gotten a booty call earlier and disappeared in a testosterone cloud. Wrench was barely able to stand on his own at that point as he eyed his truck parked in the lot.

"Wrench, you can't drive," Sharon's upstairs neighbor put his hand to the shorter man's chest to halt his progress to the car.

"Outta my way, Metro," Wrench hissed.

"Seriously, you can't drive," Metro's girlfriend jumped into the mix.

"You need to sleep it off," Sharon added.

Two others nodded in agreement.

"Bob's not here," Wrench slurred. "Place is locked."

The couple from upstairs argued in a whisper. The two roommates from the building across the parking lot slipped away.

Sharon gritted her teeth. She knew she'd be up anyway. The thought of Wrench driving his big pickup anywhere made her stomach turn. He was a disaster in the making.

"Fine," Sharon interrupted the couple, as Wrench swayed on his feet before everyone. "I'm going to be up late. Take the couch until Bob gets home. You need to stay off the road," Sharon added firmly.

Wrench smiled and wobbled his way up the stairs to her door.

"Got something to drink?" He went straight the fridge.

"No," Sharon replied, annoyed by the audacity and thankful that she hadn't stopped at the store for the extra six-pack she had planned. "Drank it all."

The swaying man continued to look into the fridge, then the freezer, even tip-toed for a glance at the top of the refrigerator.

"You done yet?" Sharon asked, hands on her hips. She was used to dealing with stupid drunks. Sharon was a police officer until two years ago. Everyone just assumed that she had always been a professor.

"Sorry, Sugar. Thirsty." The man slurred the words.

"I'll get you water," Sharon stepped into the kitchen. "Couch is there." Sharon pointed to the brown sofa. "I've got reading to do. I'll keep an eye out for Bob. When he gets here, you're gone."

Wrench sat on the couch. He took the water and downed half of it.

"This has no kick." He held the bottle up to his eyes for inspection.

"You've had plenty of kick already. A pillow and blanket are under the table." Sharon turned to her bedroom as Wrench reached for the bedding.

The air conditioning wasn't running properly in the bedroom, and Sharon grumbled in the stuffy room. She took out a tall fan and put it in the doorway. The door was barely cracked to let the air move. Sharon pulled out her reader and continued the book from the previous night. She fell asleep while reading.

Sometime in the middle of the night, Sharon heard water running. Her first thought was rain. It didn't sound like drops though. It was more focused, like a stream. She laid there with her eyes closed and inventoried the apartment. *Shower? No. Sinks? Sounded similar, but no. Dishwasher? No. Washing machine? Don't have one yet.* Finally, she had to address it.

She opened her eyes and swung around to let her legs hit the floor. They were still inches from the carpet when her brain registered the scene.

Next to the fan in her doorway, stood Wrench in all of his glory. Head leaned back. Hands on his manhood. A solid stream shooting straight in the fan as it moved side to side.

"What the...!" Sharon shouted.

Wrench bolted back to consciousness.

His mouth started moving, "Sorry, Sugar had to go. Had to go, Sugar."

"Jackass! You had to walk past the bathroom to pee on that fan." Sharon stood and glared. "Get! Out!" She shouted and pointed to the door as she started backing the drunk towards the door.

Wrench backed through the kitchen, past the bathroom, across the living room. He glanced at the pile of clothes in front of the couch.

"Don't even," Sharon growled.

"But..."

"Out!" Sharon shouted and then realized what his hands had been holding. "Stop."

Wrench stopped reaching for the doorknob and spun back around to face Sharon.

"Touch that knob, and I'll break your hand."

Wrench stepped back, with his hands returning to where they had been. He quickly exited once she flung the door open.

"Don't move," Sharon ordered. She stepped over to the pile of clothes and kicked them through the doorway before slamming the door. She finalized it with the click of the deadbolt.

"What the...?" Her head leaned against the door.

She Did It for You

"She did it for you, you know?" The brunette growled at her sister's husband.

"What?" Lance spun to face the angry female behind him.

"Rita got pregnant for you."

"Bull, she tricked me, and look where it got her."

"You!" The brunette thrust her finger into Lance's chest. "…can be such a douche. She's in there because of you. Now that the dialysis isn't working, I have to pick up the slack. Some knight in shining armor you are. You shoulda just stayed home."

Lance stayed silent. He would break that finger off in any other circumstance.

"Rita got pregnant because the doctor said you'd probably need bone marrow if it came back again."

"That's ridiculous."

"Yeah, I agree. You treated her like crap. Still, she knew the odds are against you. You're in remission now, but you keep harping on it returning. The chances of a match are slim to none, right? You know the problem with you being such a mutt."

"I know. Talked to the doctor about that."

"After you stepped out on her," Rita's sister continued as if he hadn't spoken. "I just wanted her to kick you out on your butt. Got tired of all the 'But I love him' crap." She looked like she was ready to punch him despite the foot difference in height and the fifty pounds plus Lance had over her.

"She tricked me. Told me that she couldn't get pregnant."

"It's not that she can't get pregnant. It's that she shouldn't get pregnant. That's obvious."

"That's not the way she told it."

"Bull!" the brunette boomed. "Rita is a pain in the butt some times, but she's honest. She can't lie to save her life."

"Very funny," Lance scoffed.

"Shut up." The brunette growled. "I'm supposed to relax. If my blood pressure's sky high they won't do it."

Lance shifted his stance. He had to reign it all in. It was about the surgery this morning, not him.

In the hours following the brunette being wheeled away in a chair, Lance had plenty of time to think. He and Rita weren't going to have kids. That was clear from the start. It was actually a relief when he got sick. He didn't have to worry about putting kids and her through it all. Then he recovered, and he wasn't supposed to be able to have kids anyway. It was like a hall-pass instead of a sentence. The line of young bodies made him feel like a man again. It was fun and thrilling. It wasn't until she caught him in the truck in the park with the new office temp that he realized the mistake he'd made.

He didn't fight her on the divorce. It was nearly complete.

She never told him about the night six months ago. He called her up on a drunk dial to apologize in his alcohol haze. He was in a functional blackout by the time she showed up. The next morning, he had no idea that she had even been there, but her perfume was on the pillow. Though bizarre, he shrugged it off and figured that's where his dreams came from.

Little did he know, until a week ago at the lawyer's office, it wasn't a dream that night that had gotten him wound up. If he was to believe it was really his, like she said. She took him to bed with a mission. It didn't matter why. She had used him. She supposedly couldn't have kids either. He didn't want kids, and still she manipulated one out of him.

The hours ticked by before the doctor entered the waiting room. "Mr. Cleason?"

"Yes," Lance stood, eye-to-eye with the man in scrubs.

"The surgery went well all things considered. We couldn't save the baby. It was already too late, but the kidney surgery went well. The donor kidney is functioning properly so far. It's always good to find a sibling match. They tend to have a higher success rate. They're in recovery. It'll be a couple of hours before they are taken to their rooms."

"Thank you doctor," Lance shook the man's hand.

When the doctor was out of sight, Lance walked to the elevator. He didn't wait for the sisters to get out of recovery. He called his lawyer.

"Are the papers ready yet?"

"I was just getting everything in order. They should be ready to sign by the end of the day."

"Great. I'll be there at four," Lance stated and hung up before hearing a response.

By 4:10 that afternoon, the marriage was officially over with the swipe of the pen. "Do you have a piece of paper I can use?" Lance asked the man in the dark suit.

"I have this and this," the man held up a notepad and a stack of sticky notes.

"That'll work," Lance pointed to the little yellow squares.

He spoke as he scribbled. "Can you make sure she gets this with the papers?"

The man hesitated. Once he read the note, he nodded, and shook Lance's hand.

The papers were delivered by her lawyer the day Rita returned from the hospital. On the top of the three legal documents for her to sign was a yellow square:

I'M SORRY
FORGIVE ME
I LOVE YOU
IT'S BEST THIS WAY
I'M DOING THIS FOR YOU

Captain Meatball

The two girls waited in the car for Luke to get off of work at the sandwich shop. It was the fourth time the trio would spend the rest of a Saturday night together. For the past two months, Kathleen had driven out with Vicki during her weekends at her dad's house. Luke was the real reason Kathleen joined Vicki sixty miles away.

Luke lived a block away from Vicki's dad, and Vicki pointed him out to Kathleen on her first visit. Before that weekend ended, the trio spent a weekend at the county fair and hung out at a nearby park. Kathleen was hooked.

Luke started his job earlier in the week after football season officially ended, so the girls waited until the shop closed at nine. It seemed to take forever. He didn't walk out the door until nearly 10:30.

Kathleen jumped out of the passenger seat as Luke approached Vicki's car.

"Hey." He smiled at Kathleen.

"Hey." She beamed back and watched him duck into the backseat. Kathleen enjoyed watching the muscular seventeen year-old.

"What are we doing?" Vicki asked as she started the car.

There was silence.

"Wanna just hang out at the park?" Kathleen asked in general.

"Okay," Vicki nodded and put the car in drive.

"Fine," Luke said from the back.

Ten minutes later, the teens climbed from the car parked a block away from the park. Clinton Park was the home for many of the county's police officers, so they knew there would be a couple of park patrols since it technically closed at dusk.

The girls chatted, and Luke followed in silence behind them. They knew the best table to sit at to avoid detection and bee-lined it there. Kathleen and Vicki continued to talk but asked Luke questions when they paused.

"Tired?" Kathleen asked Luke.

"Yeah, a bit," Luke stated with heavy eyelids.

"If you don't wanna hang out, we can go."

"No, I'm good."

All three were silent.

"How did the soccer game go?" Luke asked Kathleen, but Vicki, who was also on the team, answered by describing the game.

Luke and Kathleen looked at each other while Vicki was distracted. One smile was returned with another. They looked away and looked back again.

"...so Kathleen won the game for us. It was the only goal scored," Vicki finished her story, and looked at the others. They weren't even paying attention. "Luke, you hear me?"

"What?" Luke snapped to attention.

Vicki huffed. "Kathleen won the game for us."

"You did, huh?" Luke shot his attention back to the blond at his side.

"Yeah." Kathleen blushed with her smile.

"Good for you," Luke nudged her with his shoulder.

"Ugh, I'm going for a walk." Vicki stomped off.

The two sitting on the table watched Vicki march off into the shadows.

"Congratulations." Luke said after Vicki was out of sight.

Kathleen looked up right as Luke leaned in. She had wanted to kiss him for weeks. She took a quick breath to settle the butterflies before their lips met.

He tasted like mint.

The initial contact deepened, and Kathleen followed Luke's lead without thought.

Just as it was getting good for Kathleen, Luke pulled back. He was less than a foot away. Luke's unfocused eyes were on her stomach.

Kathleen wondered, but she didn't have the chance to ask.

Luke's neck straightened before his mouth opened.

Kathleen could have never imagined what happened next.

Twenty minutes later, Vicki's car stopped in front of Luke's house, and the boy jumped out without a word.

Kathleen sat in silence. The stench filled the car. The reddish brown mess funneled down her low cut shirt. By the time the girls returned to Vicki's bedroom, Kathleen had tossed her shirt and bra in the trash. She didn't care what she looked like at that point, she just wanted the smell and ooze gone.

Vicki rushed to hand her a towel. "What the hell happened?"

"We kissed. He stopped. Then he threw up down my shirt," Kathleen growled.

Vicki laughed.

"He said, 'Sorry, I drank a bunch of rum and ate a meatball sandwich before I left work.' Dumbass!"

Kathleen stormed off to the shower.

"So, you two going out again?" Vicki snickered once Kathleen was in the bathroom.

"Not in this lifetime!" Kathleen shouted as the shower roared to life.

Old Faithful

She walked into the house for the first time in three months. She hadn't been to the family home since the funeral, even though she lived just a few blocks away. There was no real reason why she had to be there now. Her mother and sister were gone. The house was dark, stuffy and stale smelling, in contrast to the sunny and hot May afternoon outside. Maybe that was one reason why she avoided visiting. It was like the soul was gone. In fact, the heart of the home left when Dad went to the hospital for the last time.

Mom went through Dad's things quickly after his passing. Some of the things were set aside for her to take if she wanted. There was one thing that wasn't in the pile that her mom prepared. That was really why she had walked in. The flannel jacket had to be hers. Visions of Dad enjoying his outdoor sanctuary while wrapped in it make it something that she needed to have with her.

She walked down the hall and approached the doorway that was her childhood bedroom. The room was packed with stuff nearly as high as she was. A left turn had her facing her sister's old room. To the right was mom and dad's room. She started there.

A quick peek into the dressers proved disappointing. The drawers that her dad used were filled with mom's things. She turned to the closet, but his side had also been co-opted. After a deep breath, she walked back to the hall. Out of the corner of her eye, she found a stack of items that were definitely Dad's.

Just inside the doorway of her sister's old room, she found the flannel jacket that she was looking for. She wanted the blue one specifically, but only the brown one was there. Still, it was something. She held it up and smiled. She could see her dad in his outdoor reading chair, in the garage, and walking to the car for the next errand.

When the images began to fade, she sorted through the other items in the discarded pile. A shirt. Then two more. Another jacket from his favorite sports team. She continued until she got close to the bottom. Then, she stopped cold. Her hand froze and her eyes locked on it. Her throat tightened and her breathing got heavy.

More than 20 years earlier, the family – Grandma included – piled into the station wagon and left for the East Coast. It was the trip that gave her the travel bug. She loved getting up when it was still dark, having breakfast at sunrise, and driving throughout the day until they found a hotel with a pool to make her sister and her happy. The trip started before sunrise the first day of August and had lasted past Labor Day.

The first major memory came on the third day, when they drove into Yellowstone. Dad insisted on stopping to see this thing that shot water into the water every hour. He called it Old Faithful. When the motley crew crawled out of the car, she saw something in the distance across the parking lot.

"That's it," Dad told her as she pointed that way. "Let's go." He took her hand and the family walked over to the wooden benches.

They sat down, but it didn't take long before staring at the hole in the ground tested her eight year-old sensibilities. That's when she realized it was actually cold. She walked around and her dad followed her while explaining that the wait would be worth it. He helped her count down the time.

"It's August, and it's cold." She stated.

"Yeah. We're in a different place. Further north." he explained.

"It's August. It's not supposed to be cold." It seemed like an obvious point.

Dad chuckled then wrinkled his nose. He looked down at the tan sweater he wore. "Do you want my sweater?" It was the first time anyone had offered her a jacket or sweater.

"Yes." She said it with none of the hesitation that she later had when others offered their jackets.

She wrapped it around her. The sleeves far too long for her arms. The sweater wrapped around her almost two times. She sat on the wooden bench with her legs crossed. The warmth felt good, and the rest of the time seemed to fly by. Before she knew it, the water flew into the sky, and the show was over. She took her dad's hand, despite the sleeves hanging over her hands, as they walked back to the car.

The memory faded. There weren't any tears, just tightness in her chest. She pulled the sweater from the pile and immediately wrapped herself in it. She didn't know dad still had the sweater after all of these years.

As the sweater settled around her, the tightness disappeared. She no longer registered the heat of the afternoon. It had nothing to do with the weather or the house being closed. The spreading warmth was a hug through time. That's when the tears welled up.

The hallway was blurry. She barely could see the door lock as she secured it. She walked to her car under the bright sun without a second thought. The now-flowing tears subsided as she pulled out of the driveway. It took just a few minutes to get home: her home.

"Welcome home," she said to the empty house, as she shut the door behind her. "Old Faithful. You're home now."

ENDINGS

The Ends Justify the Means

Ms. Milton walked into the teachers' lounge with a spring in her step. Spring break was good, and though she hadn't taken the test yet, she knew the stick would turn pink. She just felt it, but she didn't have time this morning.

"Good morning, Ms. Milton. How are you?" the Principal asked.

"Morning. I'm good. The break was good."

"That's nice. When's your conference period?"

"Second period."

"Good. Schedule a meeting with Florence." He pointed to his secretary, who looked sick to her stomach. "Make it tomorrow."

"What's this about?" The teacher's heart instinctively pumped harder.

"We'll discuss it tomorrow." He shut the office door.

The secretary turned to her computer. "Tomorrow? Second period?"

"I guess."

The secretary leaned toward her and lowered her voice. "A word to the wise, get a union rep to go with you. That's all I can say."

"You've gotta be kidding me," the teacher muttered as she left. She had no idea where to even start. She's loved her job, did her best, and received awards for her teaching.

This isn't good. She thought.

After securing a rep for the meeting, her mind raced all day and night. She knew she'd done everything right, so there shouldn't be a problem. But…

The next morning, Ms. Milton met the union rep in the main office. "Before we go in, there are a few things that you should know," the rep began. "Everything, and I do mean everything, that you say or do will be noted. Be very careful about what you say. I can't say anything as a union observer unless they violate policies."

"Okay." Her throat tightened. *Great.* She thought. Her stomach tightened. She took a breath and followed the rep inside.

The Principal sat behind his big desk with the Assistant Principal at his side. The Principal motioned for them to sit. "Chassidy came to me because you gave her a B+ on her third quarter report card," he started.

It all clicked. Chassidy harassed her the entire week before the break. The popular honors student with connections wanted a makeup exam after walking out of class during the midterm.

"It's third quarter report card. It doesn't even go on transcripts," the teacher began. "She walked out of the exam without explanation or permission and then demanded a makeup test the next day. If she talked with me about any problems before the exam started, we may have worked out an alternative. She sat through more than half the exam before leaving. I'm sure she wants to redo her essay, like several others would like to do, but that is not possible. The rules are the same for all students, and she knew the expectations beforehand."

Both administrators scribbled notes. "Let's proceed. This is going to work as follows. I have a series of statements and questions for you. I will ask them. You will answer. Mr. Roberts will record everything. The notes will be typed, and you will sign them tomorrow. Understand."

No, not really. She took a breath. "Okay." She despite the tightness in her chest.

"One. Ms. Milton never teaches class."

Blood pounded in her head, though she really wanted to laugh at the absurdity. "With all due respect, I *teach* five classes including two college prep classes every day." She emphasized the word intentionally. "Students want to pass the exam to get college credit. My students would've complained early in the year if I wasn't teaching them. It's now April. Has anyone outside of her circle of friends complained?"

Silence.

"Two. Ms. Milton doesn't grade our work."

She took another breath. "I do grade. The English department keeps students' work in portfolios. Students have access to them, but the work remains in the portfolios. If I had known what this was about beforehand, I could have brought them for you to inspect. I could have brought my lessons plans as well."

The Principal glared at the teacher.

The accusations continued, point-counterpoint.

"...Twenty-four." The principal rattled. "We have no idea what our grades are, and when we ask to see them Ms. Milton just says 'You'll be fine'."

113

She took another breath to stop the tears that wanted to form because of the pressure of the unexpected interrogation. "Grades are part of the online system that the entire school uses. They can access their grades at any time from school or home."

She sighed.

"As far as the 'You'll be fine' comment, I say that to students who need to keep perspective about the class as a whole rather than imploding over a single assignment."

More complaints were leveled and addressed before the principal stopped. She used all of her strength to look calm on the outside, while she was breaking down inside.

Later, Ms. Milton learned that Chassidy and her friends went to the principal with more than 100 complaints, and the Principal ate it all up. The administration couldn't prove any of the claims, even after further investigation, but the Principal continued to push the issue.

The pressure hit a breaking point, with two weeks left in the school year, Ms. Milton took an emergency trip to her doctor in the middle of classes.

The ultra sound tech left to get the doctor.

He entered. "I told you that the stress wasn't good, especially in the early stages." She knew what was coming. "I'm sorry. There's no heart beat."

The principal learned of Ms. Milton's summer travel plans and advised his neighbor, Chassidy, to file a complaint with the school board the day after school ended. The school board gave the teacher 48 hours to justify her work, but the teacher was halfway around the world trying to recover from her loss and the stress.

Without the teacher's appearance before the board, all of the grades were reassessed by the Principal. The students got 'A's, and Ms. Milton never returned to the classroom.

Gone

The phone sounded. The number was local but not familiar. A little voice told her to pick up, though she always screened her calls. She let it go. She justified it. After a deep breath, she resumed her mixing. Cooking was her therapy. Her sanctuary, and she needed that today. She kept her mind on the bowl in front of her. It was her birthday and the one time in her life that it fell on Easter too.

Still, Max was in a hospital bed. They were high school sweethearts who married a week after graduation. No one thought it would work. People didn't understand.

The phone rang again. Same number. The voice surfaced again to pick up, but she didn't. She was lost in memories and smiling for the first time in nearly six months. Fifteen years of bliss with her best friend played on the movie screen of her mind. It made her want to see the man she loved and adored. Once more, she wanted to see the man from a year ago, not the shadow of him lying in the hospital bed. She wanted the Max before the surgeries, the tubes and monitors, the chemo, the radiation. The man who had the body of a

Greek god, the tan that showed his inner warmth and the smile that lit up her days and nights.

"Justine, you have company," her mother broke Justine's reverie.

Justice knew she was about to face something. She didn't know what, but she knew.

Max's parents stood near the door. Max's dad looked tense.

"We need to go," Max's dad began. "Got a call from the doctors. He's going."

It was a punch to the gut.

"We left him at the hospital to come for dinner. He was doing good," Max's mom said in a whisper.

The man at her side tensed more and looked away.

"The doctor called as we were getting out of the car. He's having a hard time breathing. We have to go now."

Justine felt empty. Max needed her. That was the only thing that mattered.

Without a word, Justine grabbed her purse and charged passed the couple at the door.

"We'll drive you, honey," Max's mom said. Justine didn't register the endearment from the woman who had resented her for nearly two decades. "We're going there anyway."

Justine simply walked to their car and got in the backseat. *This is the way it's going down.* She thought. Autopilot had already kicked in. She was pulled together and strong on the outside, but inside there was nothing but emptiness.

They sped along side streets dodging slow holiday drivers. The car was at highway speed well before the end of the onramp, and as they raced through the pack of cars that slowed their progress, Justine's mind wandered.

This would be the last time. She thought. *It all ends now.* She'd wished the drain of it all would go away many times during those months of balancing what had become her new reality. She didn't want it to stop this way though. She'd make sacrifices for the rest of her life if it meant Max would come home.

When they got a clear patch of highway, her heart and head screamed. *Faster! I've got to get to him now!*

Then the guilt surfaced. She was worn down, and Max knew it. He insisted that she take it easy and take the day doing what she enjoyed. She promised to visit after the Easter meal was over, and he smiled. He said that's what he wanted.

She should've gone anyway. It was the first day in the last month that she hadn't been there when the doors opened in the morning. *I'm sorry.* It was all Justine could think to say, but she remained silent in the backseat as the car raced off the highway and idled at the red light.

When the car slid to a stop at the front doors. Justine ran. She didn't care what it looked like. She took the open elevator without looking back. Justine's breathing sped up as the trip to the sixth floor seemed to take an eternity. The doors weren't completely open before Justine rushed through them, running to room 676.

"Good. I'm glad you're here," the nurse said as Justine came to a halt and grabbed her love's hand.

She looked him over and knew it wasn't good. Still, she smiled. "I'm here, sweetie. I love you."

The man under the massive mask couldn't speak. He was too exhausted. Despite that, Justine saw the relief in the chocolate brown eyes that she promised to love forever.

"He doesn't like the mask. I'll let the doctor know you're here," the retreating nurse said.

"I love you so much," Justine's eye's welled up.

The man behind the mask nodded his head and tightened his grip. Justine tried to be strong, but the façade was crumbling. Without any thought, she crawled into bed next to Max. She just wanted to hold him. Feel him.

The doctor arrived. He made no mention of Justine at Max's side. Instead, he focused on the task at hand. There was nothing more they could do. Max had signed the DNR weeks ago. Max nodded in understanding, and everything but regular oxygen and morphine was removed.

Justine got up and went to the window when Max drifted off under the medication. His parents replaced her at his side. She crawled into the window seat and put her head on her knees. There were no tears. Everything was numb.

An hour later, Max stopped his labored breathing.

Justine thought about the cruel irony as she left room 676 for the last time. Instead of her birthday and Easter of being a day of life and "He is risen", for the rest of her life they would be associated with "he is gone."

Nor Did I

The day was disastrous. Danielle rushed home after the phone call. Duke, her Border Collie, was missing. She found him, motionless, under an old oak tree. At thirty-four, she shouldn't be this upset about losing her dog, but he was the extent of her personal life at the time. Work was worse than ever. The pink slip first thing in the morning was an unwelcomed wakeup call just before the worst phone of all. Now, she had 30 days to figure out her next move and the prospects didn't look good.

The quiet and empty house got on her nerves. She didn't feel particularly social, but she definitely couldn't stay there. Danielle changed out of her work clothes and pulled on the comfort of her favorite jeans and baggy sweatshirt before grabbing her keys.

The drive to and around the lake did little to calm her unease. Danielle passed by her usual hangout with thoughts of how less than 24 hours ago she and Duke were sitting on the patio, unknowingly having their last meal together. Sure, it sounded pathetic and melodramatic, but a piece of her heart was missing. She headed home. After walking straight to the refrigerator, she popped open a beer and downed half of it before walking out to the yard.

Danielle cursed when the beer was done before she completely settled into the chair. When she went in to grab a second and heard her phone chime. It was a text from Henry, her friend and bartender. He understood that Duke was part pet, part friend, and her constant companion.

> **Henry:** Saw you drive by. You coming in tonight?
>
> **Danielle:** No. Duke died today.
>
> **Henry:** What? He was fine when you were here last night.
>
> **Danielle:** Got a call at work. Found him under a tree. Already gone.
>
> **Henry:** I'm sorry
>
> **Danielle:** Thanks. Not in the mood for people right now. Crap day. Got a pink slip before that.
>
> **Henry:** Crap
>
> **Danielle:** Yeah
>
> **Henry:** Your neighbor's here asking about you
>
> **Danielle:** Oh yay. Hope he stays.

An hour later the doorbell sounded. *So much for being left alone.* Danielle thought as she opened the door to her neighbor, Sam.

He was animated and carrying a six-pack. "Henry told me about Duke. Thought I'd come by to cheer you up."

"Thanks, but I just wanna be alone."

His shoulders slumped, and the smile faded. "How about one beer, and I'll leave the rest as a care package."

"Fine." She wasn't in the mood to fight.

His smile returned, and he strode through the door before Danielle had a chance to change her mind.

Sam began the blow-by-blow of his day without a word of prompting. She didn't care about his mountain biking excursion or his lunch date. When he started in about a woodpecker that was attacking his deck, she had to break away. The bathroom was the best option for a breather.

After a long pause and a toilet flush to cover her ruse, Danielle walked passed the dining room and slipped on one of Duke's chew toys. Before she could prepare for impact, her head hit the corner of the heavy wood table. She came to with blood flowing from the gash in her head.

"I'm good." Danielle moved to get up.

"No. You're not." Sam kept her from getting up. "There's a lot of blood."

"I just need a towel to stop it." Danielle motioned him towards he bathroom.

"We should go to the hospital. You probably need stitches." Sam handed her the towel.

"No. It'll stop. I can't afford the bill."

Five minutes later, despite her protests, Sam pulled his car into her drive for a trip to the Emergency Room. Sam worried more about blood getting on the headrest than he did about how Danielle felt. She closed her eyes. *Life just keeps getting worse.* She thought. Losing her job and her dog were completing the downward spiral. She just had her car fixed after it took a major dump, and her mom's cancer had returned. It felt like her return to Illinois was becoming inevitable.

It took an extra ten years. I worked so hard to break free. She silently screamed within her personal hell.

"You didn't hear a word I said," Sam accused while stopped at a red light.

"Um. No. Not really." Danielle opened her eyes. "I'm a little preoccupied with the hit to the head, my dead dog, the pink slip..." She trailed off. "Man, it all sounds like a bad country song." Danielle said with a sigh.

"Why don't you get over yourself?" Sam glared at her and continued in a condescending, fatherly voice. "You know, you need to stop acting like an eighteen year-old."

"Excuse me?"

"You're acting like a kid. Getting drunk. Falling down. Crying over your dead dog. Grow up already."

You have no idea about my life! Danielle's mind raced. *You barely know me. Are you kidding me?*

"Excuse me. Slipping and hitting my head doesn't mean that I'm immature. It's been a horrid day that seems to only be getting worse. You have no idea about my life, and you have no room to talk." Danielle glared Sam's way as he pulled the car in front of the ER. "You're unemployed, divorced, and have no family to speak of." She was shaking from her anger. "All you talk about is working out, mountain biking, hanging out with your friends, and sports. Talk about me being immature. Are you really fifty-something? Because, it sounds more like you're the eighteen year-old."

"It's my life." Sam replied curtly. "I didn't ask your opinion."

"Nor did I." Danielle slammed the car door and never looked back.

Sorority Girl

"Relax," the doctor stated.

Brittany took a deep breath as she lay on the table. She hoped everything would be done quickly…at least this part of it. As the doctor put the embryos in place, Brittany thought about her life. She went to her dream school but got distracted by college life her first year. The sorority, the boyfriend who dumped her at the start of summer and more made it easy for Brittany to forget that classes were the reason she was at the university.

Her parents came down on her like a ton of bricks when the probation letter arrived. Brittany had to pay her own way until she got at least a 3.0. She worked all summer while her sorority sisters traveled and enjoyed life without her. Still, Brittany didn't have nearly enough to cover tuition and expenses.

Her older sister and her brother-in-law made Brittany an offer. The couple wanted a baby, but the doctor said that it wasn't possible. Two weeks before tuition was due, they asked her to be their surrogate. At first, Brittany was horrified with the idea, but they agreed to cover all of her degree in exchange for the nine month commitment.

Brittany didn't want to waddle around campus like a loser, so she agreed on the condition that she'd stay with them in California after the fall semester. She'd get big and give birth there figuring she'd stay until she got her body back and returned to school the next fall. It sounded crazy but ended up making sense in an odd way.

"It'll be a win-win," her brother-in-law stated.

Brittany was just beginning to show when the family celebrated Christmas. Her grades improved over the fall, despite morning sickness. Still, she filed for a leave in the spring, and her parents wanted to know why. That was when her parents learned of the arrangement between the siblings and became furious.

"We want no part of this business." Dad boomed.

"But, you're going to be a grandpa." Brittany's sister protested.

"Not this way. I thought you messed things up before. Brittany! What were you thinking?" Mom interjected.

"I figured one semester would be okay. College will be paid for. They get their baby. You get a grandbaby. What's the problem? It's not like we had sex. It's their kid. I'm just the carrier."

The three left for California after Mr. and Mrs. Mulroney went silent with their children during the rest of their visit. Brittany settled into the couple's house. She tried not to be mortified by her expanding middle. Her sister started to decorate the safari-themed nursery. The pregnancy was going well. All three were at the ultrasound when the baby let it be known that he was indeed a boy. That was the fun part.

On Valentine's Day, Brittany stayed home watching TV and eating one of her latest cravings, French fries dipped in strawberry ice cream. The couple went to dinner in Malibu, and left Brittany with her feet propped up and fries ready for dipping. Brittany tried not to think about the drought in her dating life while commercials for jewelry stores, chocolate, and flowers continued to flash depressed reminders. By 8:30, she gave up and crawled into her bed in the guestroom.

The next morning, Brittany went downstairs. The house was quiet. Their car wasn't in the garage. "Guess they got a room," Brittany muttered as she explored the fridge for breakfast.

Brittany wondered what was up. Her sister worked from home as a graphic designer, so it was odd that she wasn't around. They didn't mention anything more than dinner. Brittany grabbed her phone. "Hey, you two lovebirds coming home soon? Am I on my own for dinner tonight?"

Her text went unanswered.

The doorbell rang an hour later.

"Yes?" Brittany looked at the man in the dark suit.

"Hello. I'm Detective Brown. And you are?"

"Brittany Mulroney."

"Are you related to Grant or Elaine Harrison?"

Brittany wasn't sure if it was a baby kick or her stomach tightening. "Yes, she's my sister. He's my brother-in-law."

"There was a car accident last night on the 101."

"Oh God," Brittany caught herself before her knees buckled. She took a deep breath. "Are they okay? Where are they?"

"I'm sorry…"

This time her knees did buckle.

Brittany sat on the couch. She assured the detective before he left that she was fine and that she'd call her parents as soon as possible.

She sat there.

What am I going to say? She thought.

What am I going to do? She put her hand on her protruding belly. *I can't do this.*

Brittany thought about a sorority sister who had an abortion. *That was after only a couple of months, but I'm already 28 weeks.*

I can't be a mom. I don't even have a job. I can't go to school as a mom.

Brittany tried to calm herself down with more deep breaths.

I was just going to have the baby. I wasn't gonna raise it!

Adoption?

Would mom and dad want him now? Will they even talk to me?

Am I stuck? Is my life over?

Full, body-rocking sobs began.

She pulled it together and got the hiccups under control. Brittany grabbed her phone and touched the screen.

There was a ring. Then two.

"Hello." It was the familiar voice.

"Mom..."

Ageless Character

The school's trip was cut short. The storm arrived quicker than predicted, and the ferry ride was a bumpy one.

This time, unlike the trip out to the island, the students stayed inside and below deck. A few grew green with the additional motion of the stormy seas. The group was quieter, partly from the day's activities and partly because of the rocking they were experiencing.

Duck-Young snuck a peak that the girl to his right. He had a crush on her from the moment she walked into the classroom two years ago. She wore a red jacket and had long black hair that shined even in the dim interior light.

Bae had no idea that the boy next to her dreamed of knowing her better. She was busy. She wanted to be a doctor and helped with the family at home. Bae didn't have time to think about boys.

She laughed at something her friend said and accidentally bumped into Duck-Young. "Sorry." Bae looked over her shoulder.

Duck-Young blushed when their eyes met. His voice escaped him, so he just nodded. He continued to look Bae. That was until her best friend gave him a weird look. He immediately looked away.

The boat lurched.

"Momentary delay." The speakers blared. "Please stay in your seats. We will be underway shortly." The captain added.

The teachers stood to make sure the teens followed the captain's orders. The chatter resumed.

An odd sound roared from the belly of the ferry. Talk quieted until the captain's voice sounded again. "A small mechanic problem. We will be moving shortly."

Duck-Young felt like he was leaning right. He thought it was just Bae's pull on him. He took out the ball that he carried in his pocket and played with it to distract himself. Tossing it between his hands, he got lost in thoughts of the girl beside him who smelled like flowers.

His phone sounded, and he jumped. Phones were forbidden during school hours. Duck-Young quickly retrieved his phone and peeked at the text. His brother. *Mom's birthday today.* He shut off the phone and put it back in his bag. The ball rolled to the right side of the cabin in the process.

Duck-Young got up to get his ball and got a look from a teacher. He watched Bae walk over to the teachers and overheard Bae ask the teacher to use the bathroom. His gaze followed her out into the corridor.

One of the teachers left the cabin shortly after Bae. Duck-Young knew the teacher smoked. Maybe he was sneaking one during the delay. The talk got louder as the level of impatience grew among the teens. Duck-Young joined a nearby conversation. He didn't notice the teacher's return, her face, or the heated conversation between the adults.

The captain first told the passengers to remain indoors because of the rain hitting the boat. Minutes later, the captain ordered, "Proceed quickly and orderly to the deck and get life vests. We will be lowering life boats in case."

The teachers made sure that the students behaved and walked quickly. The deck was filled with a mass of bodies being shoved together as those in the back pushed to get closer to the front. Life vests were passed back through the crowd, each of the students standing on deck slipping on one. Eventually, the vests stopped coming.

"What did I miss?" Bae asked when she caught up to her friend.

"You need one of these. Go see him." The girl pointed to a man at the front of the boat.

Duck-Young watched Bae through the crowd. He couldn't see her talking because her back was to him, but he could see the man shake his head and look down at the deck with empty hands. Bae remained there, but the man continued to shake his head. When the man looked up at the young girl again, he lifted his hand and pointed for her to go away as others surrounded him and started to plead.

Bae turned and fought her way back through the crowd to her friend, as the boat leaned further to the right. She returned with tears in her eyes. Life boats were being loaded, and Duck-Young noticed that all of people in them took life vests with them.

Panic rose in the crowd as the situation became clear. Hundreds of passengers, a handful of life boats, and no more life vests.

Bae began to cry quietly. Her friend offered to share, but Bae said no. "One vest won't work for two people."

Duck-Young knew the boat was going down quickly and the force of the storm wasn't helping matters. It was bad and quickly getting worse. He pulled the phone from his bag as he was being pushed into those around him.

I made the right decision. I love you. Happy birthday. He sent the text then tapped Bae's shoulder.

She turned around, her face covered in tears.

Duck-Young swallowed the knot in his throat. "Make you a deal."

"What?" Bae looked confused.

"I'll give you my vest if you do one thing for me."

"What?"

"A kiss." Duck-Young exhaled as the girl's eyes went wide.

Her eyes darted around and her friend laughed. "What about you?" Bae's voice was shaky.

"I'll find a boat. I'm a good swimmer, if I don't"

"Okay."

It was an awkward and prim kiss.

Duck-Young smiled and helped her into his life vest. "I liked you since the day you arrived at school." Duck-Young began. "That was my first. Thank you."

Before Bae could reply, Duck-Young stepped back into the crowd and disappeared.

When the storm subsided, Duck-Young's body was one of forty-three recovered by searchers. He was only   fourteen.

Silent Night

He moved heaven and earth to get back to the nursing home. It wasn't enough. He was sitting with his in-laws when he got the call from his cousin. "Mom's time is short."

He immediately called the airlines. Holiday travel was backlogged from storms in the Midwest and Northeast. Driving would take at least a day and a half, if he drove straight through from Orlando. On a wing and a prayer, he showed up at the airport hoping eye contact would change things to his favor. After all, she was the woman who raised him.

The agent behind the counter shrugged and apologized. No doubt it was in an effort to dismiss him. He stood his ground. The line grew with a parade of Christmas Eve travelers.

After the third dismissal and a not-so-casual comment about security on approach, an older man stepped forward from the line. "Take my ticket, if it'll help. Heard you're trying to get to San Fran. My ticket's for Vegas."

"Thanks, but I…" He waived the man off.

"Seriously, take the ticket. I'm not headed for family. Just a weekend getaway." The man offered his ticket again. "You could rent a car from there. Still a haul but doable."

The young man looked from the ticket, to the older man, and back to the ticket agent.

"You can't take his ticket, but I can ticket you for his seat," the woman behind the counter offered.

"Done." The young man stated to the woman before turning to the man. "Thank you…It means a lot."

The men smiled at each other.

"I had a mother once. Merry Christmas. I hope things work out, all things considered."

They shook hands.

After his plane landed, he dashed through the airport to pick up the car he rented through his phone while waiting to board and drove the circuitous route from Las Vegas to San Francisco. He pulled into the nursing home's parking lot. He was greeted with a foggy, cold blast of air since he had nothing with him, not even a jacket.

He raced through the building after being buzzed in and getting a visitor's pass.

The sheet was pulled over the ridges in the bed.

He let out his breath.

He was too late.

All he could do was stand in the doorway looking at the bed. He didn't hear the carolers down the hall nor did he hear his cousin's boots along the cold tile.

"She passed about twenty minutes ago." His cousin hugged him. "We had them leave her there since you were on the way."

His startled look made her take a step back.

"To pay your last respects," she added.

Flashes of his childhood played in his mind. The woman, motionless in the bed, was the mother he never knew. She had stepped up and adopted him as her own when his biological mother left. She was the one who helped him figure out a way around his dyslexia. She was the one who proofread his school work to make sure his grades remained high. She was the one who was at every track meet despite running her restaurant. She was the one who saw to it that he didn't rack up student loans as an undergrad because he had bigger things in store. She was the one who was lost to the beginning of Alzheimer's before he graduated from law school. By the time he married, she was pretty much gone.

That was two years ago, but she held on. She couldn't hold on for the last return to San Francisco though. He had just missed her.

He pulled back the sheet to see the face that had showed him love. He took the cold hand in his and slumped into the seat next to the bed. The tears flowed freely now. He hunched over and kissed the hand knurled by arthritis. His forehead rested on her hand.

A half hour later, he summoned the strength to stand up.

"I love you." He whispered as he pulled the sheet back into position.

His cousin stood at the door. "It was beautiful really," she started. "Christmas was always her favorite holiday. She passed just after midnight. She made it to Christmas."

"That's good," he replied out of courtesy. He was numb.

"As she passed, the carolers came down the hall singing 'Holy Night'. I know it was her." She smiled.

The two hugged and the carolers returned down the hall. As they passed the room, they softened their singing. He heard 'Angels We Have Heard on High', and he knew that he hadn't missed her after all.

It's Mutual

Jessica thought about it for a couple of weeks. It didn't feel right anymore. She was ready to move on. There were others showing interest in her, and their interest excited her. As that feeling grew, the lack of excitement about Glen grew as well. He was good on paper. He was tall, fit, and good looking. He had a great job and his own house. The extracurricular activities were fun, but still she could only say it was ho-hum overall.

She changed out of her work clothes and put on clothes to go out. No need to impress tonight. Jessica kept it acceptable but didn't go out of her way. Black jeans, cream colored blouse, and the boots that gave her an attitude. *That'll keep me on point.* She thought.

Jessica grabbed her jacket, purse, and keys before locking the door. It had been a while since she met Glen for dinner. She preferred it this way. It gave her an easy out. She could leave when she wanted.

Once on the highway for a quick drive down to the mall, Jessica's mind reviewed her plan. She'd wait until after dinner. It's not that she was trying to get a last free meal. It seemed more logical to let the meal play out first since they'd both made the effort to go to dinner.

She exited the highway and then made her way through the parking lot, easily finding a space in front of the restaurant. She strode to the door with the added boost of the sound of her boots hitting the pavement.

Go with focusing on work. She thought. *If he calls B.S. then it's I'm not happy and want some space. Typical guy line...It's me, not you. At least he doesn't have stuff at the apartment. Already clear my stuff from his house. It'll be clean. I hope.*

Jessica reached for the door and took a deep breath. She was good with it. It just sucked to make people unhappy.

Glen greeted her in the bar. "I have our name in. It should be called any minute. I wanted a beer. You want a drink?"

"Sure." She situated her purse, as Glen motioned to the bartender. She smiled as the woman approached. "Vodka tonic, please."

"Rough day?" Glen said before his pint touched his lips.

"No. Not really. Just getting a reset going." Jessica said casually. "You?"

"Some drama but nothing major."

They sat in silence as Jessica's drink arrived, and she took a sip. *This is gonna be tedious.* She thought. She tried not to jump too fast or smile too big when the hostess came to tell them the table was ready. Glen closed the tab as Jessica followed the hostess.

Once seated, the menu gave Jessica an easy excuse to avoid conversation. She was familiar with the menu, but studied it like it was brand new. Jessica glanced at Glen across the table. He seemed to be intent on his menu as well. Jessica exhaled and took another drink before raising the menu high again.

Ten minutes later, the orders were placed, and the menus were removed. It became a series of comments and small talk. There was no mention of the upcoming weekend. Jessica was glad. Avoiding that topic would make things easier. The arrival of her dinner salad was a welcomed additional excuse to remain relatively quiet. Jessica drew out her salad until the entrees arrived.

When the dinner plates were as clean as they were going to get, both sat back in their chairs. Her stomach fluttered ever so slightly. She knew it was right, but she just dreaded the idea that it might become a debate. *How telling.* Jessica thought as she hoped her relationship of a year and a half would end without a fight.

Jessica opened her mouth and began without any further delay. "Glen, there's something I need to say..."

"There's something I want to say to you, first." Glen downed the last of his beer and gripped the edge of the table with his straightened arms.

Jessica opened her mouth to speak, but Glen shook his head.

"I've been doing some thinking." He started. "You are an amazing woman. You're the whole package, but..."

Don't smile. Don't smile. Don't smile. Jessica repeated as Glen took a deep breath and struggled with his wording.

"...I think I need to take a step back from this." His finger waved back and forth between him and her. Glen looked at her wearily.

She flashed a huge smile. "Thank God."

Be Careful What You Wish For

He never saw it coming. Neil woke up on Tuesday feeling like he was on top of the world. He had the car, the house, the girl, and the investment career that allowed him to get anything else that he wanted. He was the youngest to head a major investment fund. Neil was the man others were either completely jealous of or wanted to be.

Law enforcement swarmed like bees into the office as Neil made his way into work. Everything was locked down and confiscated. His name was at the top of the list as responsible parties for shady trading practices. He knew did everything right, but his gut told him there was more to the situation than he knew.

Neil left his Adelaide office and drove home on autopilot. His mind wandered after the drama of his exit. The biggest challenge of the day was getting to his car and getting out of the parking garage. The media smelled a drama and were hungrily stalking the stars of the latest scandal.

A small group of reporters met him at his house, and Neil knew he had to get out of town. *Sydney?* He could use some advice from his father and the calm of the family home. A fourteen hour drive seemed like a good way to insure that he would be left alone. It sounded good, but it didn't sound right.

Neil opened the door to the quiet house. *Thank God Liz is in Singapore until tomorrow.* He didn't want to face her and the questions that he had no answers to anyway. He began packing a bag. Sydney was logical. Getting away from Adelaide was a given.

It took less than ten minutes. He went to the desk.

> *Liz,*
> *Needed to get away. Don't know why they are investigating me yet, but I need to get out for a bit to figure things out.*
> *See you soon.*
> *Neil*

He left the note on the kitchen counter and headed out to his car. Neil kept the windows up until he cleared the crowd out front. *I wish I could just disappear.*

When it came time to commit to the road out of Adelaide, he took a different route. *Time for a walkabout.* He thought. Instead of heading to the east and his family in Sydney, Neil headed northward. Neil punched his GPS. It would be nearly the same amount of time driving. He'd always wanted to see it but never had. No one would look for him there. He headed for the Northern Territory.

As the sun dipped low to the west, Neil refueled the car. He bought water and snacks for the road. When the man behind the counter told him there wasn't much past that point, Neil sat down for a meal. He was glad to eat in relative silence, as only a few people entered or left.

He continued heading north into the dark. The man had warned him about the dangers of driving the road to Alice Springs. Neil laughed as he replayed man's words. "That road is dangerous. Nothing around. Drives some people crazy"

"I'm already going a bit crazy." Neil muttered to himself.

He was in a full life review within twenty minutes of resuming his drive. Neil always did want was right…what was expected. By all accounts, he was an upstanding man with the successful life to prove it. Even as a boy, he focused on doing everything to insure success. The right schools, the right classes, the activities, the right contacts. Where did that get him now? Instead of giving Neil the fight to make things right, the drive was dropping him into a pit of doubt.

Well into the night's darkest hours, Neil's eyes began to feel heavy. The adrenaline of the day took its toll. There was nothing on the horizon. He rolled down the window to get some air moving. It worked for a few minutes before Neil's head actually nodded. "That's it." Neil muttered. "I don't have a death wish. I just want to disappear."

There were a few hours before daybreak, so Neil pulled off the road a safe distance. He'd get a couple of hours before finishing the trip into Alice Springs. At some point he'd get to Uluru. *Hopefully, I'll avoid the tourists and everyone else. I just want to disappear.*

Neil stretched the seat back and drifted off. He quickly dropped into a dream state. Before him stood Uluru, Ayers Rock. The day advanced in fast forward before him from sunrise to twilight. At some point, he realized that he was no longer himself. He was an Aboriginal, and this was his home. He watched the people flock to the site and cover the landscape like ants with nothing more than the desire for a picture to note a checkmark on their bucket lists. The sense of anger and injustice grew. It became a ball of white-hot light encompassing everything.

While Neil was lost in his dream, a bright streak appeared in the sky. Many people from a vast area took pictures and video of the trail headed across the darkness. The images were plastered worldwide throughout for the next 24 hours.

The crater left by the impact in the Outback would also be located and documented. The one thing that would never be properly noted was the fact that before the crater formed, a car with a lone sleeping man, was occupying that spot.

He never saw it coming.

It seemed to everyone that Neil simply disappeared into thin air. It made him an even more appropriate scapegoat. For decades to come, the life of Neil would be the subject of many rumors and tales. Though he literally vaporized, Neil remained at the top of the most wanted lists for white collar crime in Australia and worldwide.

BEYOND

10:14

Tom sat at the table in the restaurant across the street from his hotel, gulping down the cold beer he needed desperately. The last minute business trip hadn't gone as planned. More busy days were ahead. Yes, he should be happy. He was happy. More Happiness was to come. Tom knew he'd spend the rest of his life with her from the moment they bumped into each other at the coffee shop. He didn't care about a June wedding. That's what made her happy though. It would be more enjoyable for them both if she had agreed to delay everything until this project was completed.

Tom sighed. The older man to his right chuckled. Their eyes met over polite, awkward smiles.

"Tough day?" The silver haired man asked.

"Yeah, and heading back to a hornet's nest tomorrow." Tom's shoulders slumped.

"That doesn't sound good." The man took a drink of his soda.

"It's good...great really. Just the timing sucks."

"Life's about the moments. Remember that the present is a real present. When it's gone, you'll miss it."

147

"There's no way I'll miss it. I'd never live it down," Tom took a drink.

"Let me guess. It involves a woman." The man smiled.

"Sure does. Big day."

The man smiled bigger and sat up straighter. "Well, congratulations then." He turned to the passing waitress. "Make it two of those." He pointed to Tom's pint. "We have some celebrating to do."

The two began passing the time by talking about plans for the honeymoon. They went down the memory lanes of misspent youths and laughed at the fact that the same themes came up in both of their lives.

After two more beers, the older man got up. "I'm not as young as I once was. Nine o'clock's midnight to me now. Travel safe and enjoy the moments ahead. I wish you and your bride the best."

"Thanks," Tom said with a smile and shook the older man's outstretched hand.

"Before I go...may I be the first to give you a wedding present?"

"Ahh, well." Tom tried to figure out what to say.

"I don't have family anymore, and I want to pass something on." The man explained and pulled his hand from his pocket. He had a shiny yet old pocket watch in his hand. "My dad gave this to me on my wedding day. It was his dad's too."

"I couldn't..."

Tom's protest was cut short with a wave of a hand. "Let it remind you to live in the moment. Consider it a good luck charm. It's seen three long, happy marriages and brought its owners home safely from three different wars." He placed both hands around Tom's outstretched one. "To a long, happy marriage and always arriving home safely." The man smiled and walked away.

"Thanks," was all that Tom could get out as the man disappeared out the door.

The next day, Tom was in line at the airport. It looked like security would take as long as his five hour flight would. After the line finally inched up to the point that Tom handed over his license and boarding pass, he pulled out his laptop and put his carry-on bag on the belt. As he kicked off his shoes to place them in the bin, he checked his pockets. Loose change, a pack of gum, his wallet, several of his business cards, and the silver watch dropped into the bin. The watch popped open, and Tom went to quickly close it before going through the machine.

10:09. Great... Tom thought and nearly growled. *I've got 10 minutes to make it to the gate.*

Two minutes later, he passed through the body scan. He scrambled to collect his belongings. Tom hustled to the end of the terminal and found the plane was boarding. Tom was three people away from the ticket scanner when he heard the announcement.

"Passenger Tom Dalrymple please report to checkpoint three." He doubted his hearing until the same words repeated over the speaker.

"Damn it." He muttered under his breath and worked his way through the wall of humanity that pushed towards the gate. *Just great. Gonna miss the flight now. What the heck?*

He got to the checkpoint and pulled a screener aside. "My name is Tom Dalrymple. There was an announcement for me to return here." The screener went over to a woman at a podium.

The woman motioned him over. "Are you the owner of a pocket watch?"

"Uh," Tom fumbled in his pocket and realized it was missing. "Yes, a silver one."

The woman handed it to him. "You forgot it in a bin."

"How did you know it was mine?"

"There was a business card with it." She stated.

"Thank you."

The door was closed to flight 1014. Tom walked to the counter, explained the situation, and rebooked for a flight that was three hours later. He found a seat at a crowded restaurant and settled down to a burger and beer. He watched the games on the TVs. One beer became two after leaving a voicemail to tell his bride that he would be later than planned.

His phone rang as the second beer arrived.

"TOM!" The voice screamed before he could say hello.

"Yes. Hon, what's wrong?"

"Oh my god! You're okay?"

"Yes. Why wouldn't I be?"

"Your flight...Flight 1014 crashed. It's on TV."

When Tom was able to speak, he calmed her before ending the call. He took the final slug of his beer and fumbled for his wallet. The watch came out with it. When he looked at the dial, he was silenced once more.

The arms were motionless. 10:14.

The Visitor

NOTE: This story was first published by Janelle Jalbert in *Flash Fiction* online magazine.
*** *

It was dark. The snow continued to pile up outside the apartment window. It was peaceful watching the white curtain turn amber in the glow of the streetlights. Still, Gabriella was tired of the snow, the cold, and the late nights finishing up her research. Thanks to technology, her due date was firm, even if the streets in Madison, Wisconsin were impassable in the morning.

Gabriella's mind wandered. Fourth of July.

She and Uncle Charlie were living it up at the family reunion, crafting icy concoctions to battle the humid heat in Virginia. Pitchers slushed as they were passed. Loud laughter was everywhere. Uncle Charlie was singing her praises about her doctorate. Gabriella soaked it in, despite her shy nature.

"My little Gaby is going to be a PhD!" He shouted and toasted.

"Okay already." Cousin John grumbled. "What's the big deal?"

151

"Excuse me?" Uncle Charlie stared at his son.

"Why don't you just fess up already?" The younger man glared.

"Stop it." Uncle Charlie growled back.

"Let's just call it as it is already." John took a breath and sneered. "You gush over her out of guilt."

"Stop." Charlie growled.

"Hey everybody!" John stood. "The reason my dad here is so happy for Gaby is because he's guilty that he gave her up."

John squared his shoulders to his dad "She was an inconvenience to his career. Her mom was a lapse in judgment that led to the ultimate mistake. I'm not really his first born. She is." John pointed to Gabriella

Gabriella sat in stunned silence, the redness on her face a combination of heat and humiliation.

"Following in daddy's footsteps. Even if you didn't know who your real daddy was."

Gabriella sighed as she stepped away from the wintry window. It took months for her rational mind to penetrate the hurt as the pieces came together. Uncle Charlie, dad, had an affair with another VP in the office. From that, she was conceived. Neither was willing to take on a baby then.

Charlie also had Aunt Reina to contend with, which explained the weird looks every time Gabriella talked with the woman. Still, Uncle Charlie had helped his sister and husband. Mom, as Gabriella knew her, had leukemia as a child and was told that she'd never have kids. Gabriella had always been told she was a miracle. She just hadn't known the miracle involved other biologicals.

Gabriella returned to her computer and the mountain of research printouts. Focusing on the final check of her research was the best way to occupy her mind. As the night, now morning, edged closer to three, Gabriella was fully charged on caffeine and engrossed in her work. Everything was quiet, except for her fingernails on the keyboard.

Knock, knock, knock.

It was relatively faint but caught Gabriella's attention anyway.

Next door. She thought.

KNOCK. Knock. Knock.

Gabriella turned towards the sound. *Not next door.*

She got up despite knowing that no one would drop by on a night like this, at a time like this, and especially this night in particular. She had hung the Do Not Disturb sign out on life. She said it was in order to finish of her research, but the reality was more than that.

Three o'clock in the morning? In a snow storm? Who? What the...?

Gabriella looked through the peephole.

Uncle Charlie...Dad...stood in the hallway.

She unlocked the door and opened it.

"Surprise," Charlie smiled.

"Uh. Hi." Gabriella stammered. "How did you get here? I mean, what are you doing here? Why?"

Charlie smiled. "Oh Gaby. I had to see you first."

Gaby's brain seized. She stayed silent as he crossed the threshold.

"Are you okay, Gaby?"

"I guess." She crossed her arms. "I don't understand."

"I wanted to tell you that I am so proud of you and all that you're doing."

"Okay."

"You need to understand. You were always wanted. You were never a mistake. You really were a miracle."

"Okay," Gaby was getting a sick feeling.

It was something about the word 'were'.

"You came here. Now. To say that?"

"Had to make sure you heard it from me. You were always wanted, and you will always be loved more than you can imagine."

Gaby stepped back and looked Charlie in the eye. "Okay, but I don't understand."

"You will," Charlie smiled.

Gaby stiffened. *This doesn't make sense.*

"I've got your graduation present." Charlie smiled and looked into the eyes that were mirrors of his own.

"I don't graduate for months, and I won't if I don't get things done tonight." Gaby stiffened.

"I've gotta give it to you now. At least tell you. You've always wanted to go to Hawaii, right?"

She nodded.

"I got you tickets for May, and my beach house on Maui is all yours…for as long as you want it."

"Thank you, but still. You could've waited to tell me."

"I had to tell you now. Know that I have always loved you and always will."

She wanted to say it back, but it stuck in her throat. "Okay."

Charlie smiled at Gaby through his disappointment. "I'll always be there for you. Just ask."

He gave her a soft kiss on the forehead that felt as light as air and walked out the door.

Just as the door closed, she spun to open it again. *There's no way he could get anywhere in the snow,* she thought.

"Charlie!" she shouted out into the hallway. "You can't...."

She looked right. She looked left. No one was in the long hallway.

"I love you," Gaby whispered as she shut the door.

Minutes later, Gabriella's cell phone came to life.

"Gabriella, it's Aunt Reina. Sorry it's late, or early. I'm calling because..."

Gaby inhaled.

"...Charlie died an hour ago. Massive heart attack."

Roadside Assistance

Monica was well into her drive. She had to be in Memphis for her job interview in less than 24 hours. She knew April weather could be questionable on highway 40. Still, the snow surprised her.

Monica debated about stopping in Albuquerque when the flurries started. She pushed on. The trip was a familiar one. She aimed for Santa Rosa, about a hundred miles east. Once she topped the Sandia Mountains outside of Albuquerque, she was committed.

Thirty miles later, she picked up a car with New York plates in front and a New Mexico one in back. Tucked in. She breathed a bit easier. "Ok, New York. If you're going, I'm going," she muttered.

The snow mounted on the highway.

Her New Mexico helper got off the highway at a truck stop. Still, she stayed tucked in the tire tracks of New York.

A little more than two hours later, the pair of eastbound cars made the sweeping turn into Santa Rosa, the highway remained open. New York continued through town without slowing.

"Okay, onward it is." Monica did some quick math and figured the next stop would be Tucumcari. That would be it. She'd get a room, take a well-deserved hot shower, and relax.

The state troopers moved the large metal bars in Santa Rosa across the highway a mere three minutes after the two cars passed.

A half hour later, it became into blizzard conditions. The white hitting the windshield made Monica nauseous as she got a taste of vertigo. The faint red lights ahead of her faded. Then, they disappeared from view completely. She was on her own.

Monica slowed the car even more as the wind kicked up with the heavier snow. She knew better than to stop. The little girl in her screamed to make it all go away.

That moment of distraction was all it took. A crosswind hit her SUV and pushed it hard right. The SUV came to an abrupt stop in the snow on the side of the road.

Monica came to the harsh realization that the all-wheel drive wasn't going to do her any good. She prayed that any cars behind her wouldn't swerve her way because of her blinking hazards. It was cold and probably only going to get cooler. At least she had more clothes, blankets, water and protein bars.

The first headlights, since her New Mexico driving companion turned off, appeared through the white curtain of snow. She realized it was a tow truck as it pulled alongside. Instead of being the guarded city gal when the man trudged over and knocked on her window, she flung the door open.

"Got blown off the highway." She stated to the man who stood at least a foot taller than her in his blue uniform.

"How'd you get here? Highway's been closed for a while."

"Wasn't closed when we went through Santa Rosa." Monica replied.

"We?" The man's brow shot up as he looked around her into the SUV.

"I was following another car."

"They didn't stop?"

"Didn't know them. They disappeared before it happened." Monica explained.

"You go and sit in the truck. It's warm. There's a thermos of coffee if you want some. I'll see what I can do." The man began to assess the situation around the SUV.

Monica never questioned her safety. Later, she would wonder why. She simply climbed into the cab of the tow truck and warmed her hands in front of the vent. The truck was silent except for the sound of the warmth through the vents and the engine running. Monica sighed after realizing that she had been holding her breath. The reality was she hadn't breathed comfortably since before Albuquerque, but her stubborn side had taken charge. Now, all she could do was wait, hope for the best, and breathe.

The man returned to the truck, put the truck in reverse, maneuvered it back, and jumped out again.

The next time he jumped in, he put the truck in drive. After a few moments of spinning wheels, the truck lurched forward.

Ten minutes later, Monica returned to her SUV which was back on the highway. "Thank you so much," Monica smiled. She handed him the last twenty in her wallet. "I wish it was more."

"No problem ma'am. Glad to help." The man waved it off and smiled. "You better get going. Stop in Tucumcari. The storms supposed to get worse before it gets better. I'll lead the way."

"You don't have to…" Monica started.

"I'm going that way anyway. You have a phone?"

Monica nodded with a bit of dread. The last thing she wanted now was to get picked up.

"Good. Here's my card." The man handed her the rectangle. "If we get separated or you run into trouble before town. Call that number. I'll circle back around."

Monica let out a breath. "Thank you."

The next morning, Monica awoke to sunny skies outside of her motel room in Tucumcari. She dressed and went to a truck stop diner for breakfast. She looked at the business card in her wallet as she paid her bill. The address on the card was only a block away. Monica found the A & H Towing sign quickly and turned into the lot.

"Can I help up?" The man asked.

"Yes, one of your drivers helped me on the highway last night. I just wanted to thank him."

The man's brows furrowed, and he shook his head. "That's impossible ma'am. We weren't out last night."

Monica's head jolted back. "But, I have his card." She pulled out the business card with the name MICHAEL SMITH printed on it.

The man took it from her and looked it over. "I don't know what to tell you ma'am. Only two drivers here. Me, Jose Martinez, and my son, Angel Martinez. There's no Michael Smith here. Never has been."

I'm Here

Elisa sat on her apartment balcony drinking coffee on the biggest morning of her life to date. Today was graduation day. All the time, energy, and money that she didn't always have was about to pay off. In less than four hours, she was going to be a college graduate. She sighed. *I wish you were here, mom.* The bittersweet moment mixed with the last of her coffee.

One more cup won't hurt. She slid the door open, walked through the bedroom, looked at the hanging gown, and returned to the coffeemaker. Once her mug was set, she reversed course back to the balcony.

"What the…" she asked when she saw her chair.

The lone blue plastic patio chair in the small balcony was covered in small, white, fluffy feathers. She slid the door open and looked around for the poor bird. No doubt there was a carcass to be found given the amount of feathers. "There's no way that bird survived," she muttered and wondered if the neighbors got a cat.

There was no cat. There was no carcass. In fact, she didn't see a single bird or hear from one either.

Elisa brushed the soft feathers from her chair and sat. Her thoughts returned to her mom. The woman raised her all by herself. They were a team right up until those last breaths four months ago. Mom insisted that Elisa finish her classes despite the fact that the diagnosis was bad, and time together was short. It had been a challenge to care for mom, make it to class, find time to study, and still keep the job that made it all possible. Her mom kept her going. Her mom handled two jobs and their lives, and Elisa had no doubts about returning the favor once she got the news.

The cough plagued mom for a long time. The fire in her mom had slowly faded over the last couple of years. Both thought it was just fatigue. It wasn't until Elisa stopped one day and really looked at her mom and watched her move, that she saw how old the forty-two year-old looked that something told her that things weren't right.

Three months later, Elisa stood at the edge of the ocean and let her mom fly freely. It was her mom's dream to travel and see the world. When Elisa arrived the day after her mom's 17th birthday, those dreams were tucked away for good. Elisa opened the box and let the dream become a reality 25 years later.

"Man, mom, I wish you were here to see it today." She thought about how fragile and worn her mom looked in the last days and knew it was better that mom wasn't suffering. "I'm happy you're free and comfortable, but geez, I wish I could have you there just for a few minutes. I know you'd be so happy. Just like you wanted. I'm the first to get a college degree."

Elisa finished her coffee and stretched in the chair before getting up. The wispy white feathers at her feet caught her eye as they floated around with the breeze. Something about them made her smile. With that grin, Elisa got up and readied herself for the moment she had waited and worked for all this time.

Two hours later, Elisa and her best friend Maya parked and made their way to the area set up for the ceremony. Maya helped Elisa slip into her gown and get the cap just right on her head. "Thank you so much for coming to see me do this today," Elisa stated.

"Of course, wouldn't miss this for anything. You're faaabulous!" Maya opened her arms wide for a hug as the two laughed.

"You're the only real family I've got now," Elisa said over Maya's shoulder.

"You betcha, sister. Always. I got your back," Maya smiled as they ended the hug. "Now let's get this show on the road! First we gotta get a picture of all this fabulousness."

Maya pulled out her phone and snapped away. An unsuspecting passerby got recruited to take some pictures of the two. They hammed it up and did some proper shots before letting the recruit go about his day.

As Elisa stood to walk towards the stage with the others, she looked back to the crowd. It was amazing to see the mass of people. She couldn't see Maya in the audience, and there was only the briefest moment that Elisa felt a tug with the wish that she had someone else to look for among the faces. With a deep breath, she followed those around her to the stage. She took the stairs, heard her name, walked to shake the hand, and took the slightest second to pause. "I did it!" she said to herself with one of the biggest grins that she'd ever had.

The walk back to her seat got her again. "Mom. I did it. I wish you were here." The graduates made their way down the row of chairs to be seated once more. Elisa looked at the cover in her hand as she followed the person ahead of her. When the line stopped, she looked over to her seat. There was a large white feather resting on her chair. Again, there wasn't a bird to be seen. She grabbed it before sitting. It was the length of her hand and perfectly shaped. She twirled it and studied it as the names continued to be announced from the stage. At the end of the ceremony, Elisa and Maya found each other among the mass of jubilant humanity.

"It's the craziest thing," Elisa stated after the initial shrieks, jumping, and hugs. "I found this feather on my chair when I came back from the stage."

Maya nearly jumped when Elisa showed her the feather. "Oh girl!"

"What?"

"Elisa, you don't know?"

"Know what?"

"That's your mom saying 'I'm here'."

The Talking Board

Shannon had never heard of an Ouija board before she walked into the sleepover. Four girls huddled on the floor with their hands on a teardrop looking piece of plastic moving over a brown board filled with letters. Shannon dropped her bag in the other room and joined the others in front of the couch.

"Hey, Eva brought it," Annie stated as Shannon sat down on the floor with the two onlookers.

"What is it?"

"A Ouija board."

Shannon had a blank look.

"You ask it a question, and it spells out an answer," Annie explained.

Shannon didn't see how one answer was possible with four people moving the piece. The four attached to the board were spelling out an answer to a question that Shannon hadn't heard. Then there was a squealing chorus.

"You're gonna get with Robert!" Dana shouted at Courtney.

Courtney countered with a new question. "What's up with Dana and Zac?"

The girls got quiet and focused on the board once more.

D-A-T-E the board spelled out.

"How did it know?" Dana shouted again. All of the girls in the room looked at Dana. "He asked me to Homecoming today."

"I knew it!" Courtney shouted before getting up and heading to the kitchen.

"Who spelled it out?" Shannon asked.

"Spirits," Anne replied. "It's a spirit board. Connects you to the other side. Gotta be careful with it though. You have to ask the right questions."

"What are the right questions?" Shannon asked.

"They have to be specific, and you have to end every time by moving the thing over Goodbye."

"What happens if you don't?"

"The spirit sticks around." Annie shook her shoulders like she had the chills. "That's just creepy."

Shannon was still skeptical, but took the spot Courtney vacated. The four girls seated around the board put their hands in place. No one said a word.

Then Dana asked, "Who is Shannon going to date?"

Shannon was shocked to feel the reader begin to move. She tried to figure out who was pushing it, but the motion didn't seem to come from any one direction. It just moved.

S-T-E-V-E

"Who's Steve?" Dana asked while others waited for Shannon to answer.

"Don't know," Shannon shrugged. "I don't know a Steve."

The girls looked disappointed. "Doesn't work every time," Dana explained.

Unimpressed, Shannon got up to join Courtney in the kitchen.

Two hours later, the novelty of the board had worn off. It sat ignored on the coffee table as the girls moved on to other entertainment. Shannon looked at it. She walked over and sat in front of it. She wanted to see if it really worked or if the others were just pulling a trick. Shannon moved it closer and put her fingertips on the pointer. She didn't say a word but thought about her question.

Am I going to college?

The pointer moved to the top corner and pointed to YES.

That's a no brainer. She was an honor student after all. *Where?*

G-E-O-R-G-E

"George?" Shannon muttered, ready to give up, but the pointer kept going.

T-O-W-N

"Whoa, Georgetown? Never thought of that one," Shannon paused. Her brain worked on another question. Shannon's parents were worried that she was hanging out with the wrong friends, and there she sat with a Ouija board that would have sent her religious dad into a meltdown. That made her remember his promise to her the day before. If she got good grades, he would send her on a trip to the place she always wanted to go: Australia. Shannon was excited by the idea, but also knew her dad. She doubted he would pay for the trip, even though good grades were a given.

Where am I going for my graduation trip? Shannon asked silently.

S-Y-D-N-E-Y

"Okay then..."

The pointer continued to move. B-A-D

"Bad."

G-U-Y

"Guy. Who?" Shannon whispered.

T-R-A-V-I-S

"I don't know a Travis," Shannon said with annoyance.

"Hey, you're not supposed to do that alone. It's really bad if you do." Courtney explained with a frown.

"Worked fine for me." Shannon said as she pushed the board back on the table. She made sure that the pointer floated over 'Goodbye' before she lifted her fingers. "Thought we were walking to the movies."

"We are." Courtney stated. "Let's go."

Shannon never played with a Ouija board again. In fact, the thought of it didn't return until the summer after her high school graduation trip.

The group of girls decided on Mexico. Mazatlán, specifically. Shannon remembered her dad's promise. There was no way she'd forget when she had a poster of Sydney Harbor on her bedroom wall. She was off to Georgetown in the fall and knew money was tight. She figured Mexico was cheaper than Australia and joined her friends south of the border.

Four days into the Mexican vacation, a new friend from Northern California introduced Shannon to Travis. Later that night Travis attacked Shannon. It wasn't until she was home again, recovering, that she remembered where she had heard the name Travis before.

She shuttered. "I thought the bad guy was in Sydney, so Mazatlán was safe."

Then she remembered her boyfriend sophomore year, a soccer player named Steve. Shannon's stomach turned, as she realized she was also headed to Georgetown.

Six years later, Shannon graduated with a Masters degree. She started her undergraduate work at Georgetown but left after a year. Shannon finished her degree at a state school before going to a private university in San Diego for her graduate work.

Three weeks before summer vacation ended and Shannon was due back in the classroom for her second year of teaching, she got an email about a discount deal on airfare to Sydney. It ended up being her graduation trip.

Airborne

Sergeant Raines pounded his fist at the door; wadded up the paper; and stormed back to his car. The key was shoved in the ignition, and the car roared to life. He sped down the drive leaving a trail of gravel and debris in his wake.

How could she? He thought. *We've planned this for six months, and she waits until I'm stateside. Four years...wasted.*

He made his way down the narrow, windy road to the highway. He didn't know where he was going, but he sure as hell wasn't staying in the town where he was supposed to have gotten married. He drove on autopilot as he replayed the events in his mind. He didn't have the patience to handle all the sight-seers on the main road and took a right to use the back way down the mountain.

The sun had dipped, leaving the lake and the surrounding communities in the fading evening light. It was a clear evening after the previous day's snow. The route along the lake's north shore was more tenuous, so tourists tended to stick to the main road once colder

171

weather arrived. It was fine with him. He didn't notice as the scenery flew by. Without traffic, it was easy him to lose his sense of speed.

He tires barked and squealed on a hairpin and brought his attention back. The focus remained for a matter of minutes before the image of the writing flash before him. *This is the hardest thing I've ever had to do, but...*

The car picked up speed again. *...It was a mistake, and I have to do what's right for the baby and me. He's a doctor and has a stable practice and a home...*

A woman in a SUV sat overlooking the lake trying to get a few minutes of quiet before heading home and tackle mommy duties. She took a deep breath, sighed, and moved to turn the key. "Time to get this show on the road."

The SUV inched towards the road, she looked left and then right. That's when she saw them. Three deer stood in the middle of the road, right at the apex of Dead Man's Curve. She watched for a moment and prayed, for both the deer and any driver who may be coming from the other direction. It was virtually a blind curve.

She noticed movement near the deer as she hit the gas. Out of the corner of her eye, she saw it. Something flew off the cliff.

His brain was focused on Alicia. There wasn't time to hit the brakes or shift gears, figuratively or literally. Despite his training for crises as part of the 101st Airborne, he had pulled the wheel too hard.

"Shit!"

Time slowed. *So, this is how it goes.* He thought about family and the things he still wanted to do. Looks like my number's up. *If this is it, I'm good with it. It's in your hands now.*

The momentum caused the car continue straight after punching through the guardrail. The airbags blew. After the car floated out into the air, the descent began. The car did a lazy flip and landed on its roof seconds later.

The woman quickly realized it was a car launching from the road and dropping into the lake below. She slammed the brakes and reached for her cell at the same time. She gave the necessary information over the phone and raced to where the road dropped into a cove near where the car had plunged.

As she pulled to a stop, a small boat appeared near where the car bobbed almost completely submerged. In the fading light, it was hard to make out the figure with the boat, but it looked like he was trying to help. She knew how challenging it could be. She was a trauma nurse and former lifeguard. She was deciding whether it would be best to try to swim out and help, when the silhouette reappeared back on the boat. From what she could make out, there appeared to be two people on the boat now. "Maybe," She muttered. "Just maybe the driver got pulled in time."

First responders arrived, and she pointed towards the small boat. The car already sank below the surface. The officer standing next to her on the shore relayed information to a fast approaching Harbor Patrol boat. The strobe on the boat painted streaks of color around the cove as bright search lights lit up the dingy by its side.

The radio on the officer's shoulder blared. "Harbor Patrol is pulling into Darskin to transfer the vic to the hospital. EMS has been diverted."

173

"10-40. En route." The officer looked at the woman.

"I'll follow. I'm a trauma nurse."

He nodded.

The driver was unconscious when he was placed on the gurney and put into the ambulance. "That's one lucky SOB." The Harbor Master noted to the officer. "Where's Officer Michaels?" He asked. "Guy deserves a medal."

"Who?" The man in uniform asked and looked between the nurse and Harbor Master.

"Officer Michaels. He's the one with the dingy." The Harbor Master explained. "He rode here with us."

"Was he in uniform?"

"Yeah, a blue one." The man's brows wrinkled as he looked at the officer's black uniform. "Said he got the call and sped right over."

"Michaels?" The nurse asked with an odd smile as she headed for the ambulance.

"Officer Jude Michaels." The Harbor Master stated again with a touch of annoyance.

"No one on the force with that name," the Police Chief stated as she stopped beside the men.

"Mmm," the Chief muttered and grinned. "Michael the ultimate protector and warrior. St. Jude the patron saint of lost causes. Sounds like this is going to be one heck of a story."

Hugs

It was the day her grandpa was to be cremated. She decided to honor him in her own special way. She'd go into the mountains that he loved hiking in with her when she was a girl. She'd take a six pack of his favorite beer to share once she got to wherever she ended up. First, she had a stop to make though.

The ten miles to his favorite cigar shop went quick since she was going against the morning rush hour. It went fast not because of speed, but her thoughts were lost in the countless trips out to the small shop that she had taken with her grandpa. His pipe and cigar were his escape, along with a book. He was always happy to make the drive, and she loved riding shotgun to Matty's with him.

Tuesday morning meant the usual group of males reading papers, shooting the breeze, and generally escaping wouldn't be in yet. As she approached the door, a young guy she hadn't seen before ran up and held it open for her. "Thanks," she smiled as she passed.

The store was empty until they walked in. The young man walked behind the counter and put his fresh cup of coffee down. "Can I help you?"

"Oh," she said standing in front of the jar that she knew would be third from the right. It was there even after all of the months since she'd been in last. "Yes, I'd like the Grandfather's Blend, please."

"How much?" The man reached for the jar, despite the surprised look on his face.

"An ounce," she hadn't thought about it, but it came out automatically. She thought about the pipe she took out of grandpa's work truck before she left the house.

The man weighed the tobacco and sealed the bag. "That'll be eight dollars."

She handed over a twenty and waited for the change. The weight of the day began to rest on her shoulders. This would be the last time here.

She took a few steps down the sidewalk and had to do it. She pulled the plastic pouch open and inhaled deeply. The smell of her grandpa penetrated into her brain, into her heart. For a second, she forgot he was gone. He was right there.

Five minutes later, she pulled into the left lane to make her turn. The car ahead of her was slow to turn and stopped for the yellow that turned to red. Her mind was elsewhere as she sat second in line for the next green arrow. She barely registered everything around her because of what was in her head and heart.

Halfway through the cross traffic's green light, the bells went off. Then the red and white arms started their slow trip down. She came back to the moment as the arms lowered. The tracks that traveled diagonally through the intersection hadn't been used in close to twenty years. She knew that for a fact.

She looked down the tracks to the west for the railroad truck she expected. They had to be testing the crossing guards. No truck. She looked back over her shoulder to the east for the truck. The tracks were empty.

Hey grandpa. I get it. I know you're here. Glad you're happy. She thought as the arms started their ascent. *Woulda been better if I was in the middle of the intersection when they went down. It'd be like a hug.*

Her mood brightened, recognizing it for what it was. A sign from her grandpa. She smiled.

The green arrow lit, and the car ahead of her began to move forward. As she put her foot on the gas, the bells rang again. The arms came back down after she cleared the crosswalk into the middle of intersection. Once more, she looked down either side of the tracks for the reason for the crossing guards to be triggered. Again, the tracks were clear to the east and to the west.

She smiled broadly even as her eyes got watery.

"Thank you Grandpa. I felt that one."

She watched the intersection fade in the rearview as she drove back down to the highway.

The arms didn't come down again.

Reality TV Hell

Phillip Kono Jr. left his body.

"We've come for you," stated one of the three waiting for Phillip to stop looking at his old body and those who had gathered around him after the accident. He said his goodbyes. Phillip tapped the shoulders and touched the cheeks of the sad loved ones that circled the hospital bed.

An instant later Phillip Jr. stood next to Phillip Sr. for the first time in twelve years. It felt great. "Is this Heaven?" Junior asked.

Senior nodded.

"I thought there'd be a line."

Senior laughed.

"I thought that I'd have to do a life review to prove my eligibility or something."

"You came from here, so you're automatically worthy. All come from here because all are part of greatness." Senior explained.

"What about bad people, like Hitler? He was great in all the wrong ways."

"They're returned to learn more lessons from other points of view until they experience what they need." Senior plainly stated.

Junior paused to put his thoughts together. "So, everything's perfect here?"

Senior nodded.

"Everyone comes from here, and it's perfect here." Junior thought out loud.

Senior waited for the question that he knew was coming.

"Why would anyone want to leave if everything's perfect?"

"Two reasons." Senior began moving as he talked, and Junior followed. "One, perfect can get boring."

Junior stopped a moment in his surprise. *How can perfect be boring?* He thought.

"Perfection has its limitations, and sometimes souls need to learn about things or experience things for themselves rather than simply knowing them. Remember what it was like to watch TV?"

Junior nodded.

"Reality TV is such an interesting concept."

Junior didn't follow. "Why?"

"It's all the rage on Earth right now, but what people don't realize is that they are all living it."

Junior stayed silent and remained confused.

"You see. From here, Earth has been TV since the dawn of man. It's broadcasted here 24/7, though time is an Earth concept. Sometimes souls here are willing to give up things for a while for a chance to be part of the show. Just like people do in the world."

"So, life is nothing more than the ultimate reality show?" Junior asked.

"Ultimate TV show, yes. Reality, no." Senior answered.

"Life on Earth is Heaven's TV?"

Senior nodded. "Yes, we view things that can't be experienced here. There is no creation here because everything just *is*. There is no winning because there is no losing here. Those are two things that souls often want to experience from themselves."

"Interesting." Junior replied.

"There's also no fear, anger, hurt, and all of those other things." Senior continued.

"What about Hell?" Junior asked.

"Have you noticed that things are usually paired? Black and white? Good or bad? Day and night?"

"Yeah?"

"The idea of Heaven, Hell, and Earth is an interesting one." Senior mused.

"Why?"

"If everything is set up as pairs, does it make sense to have Heaven, Earth, *AND* Hell? Remember…" Senior trailed off and looked at Junior. "Everyone comes from here, and some chose to visit Earth for lessons and experience. Then, there's this random third option people describe as Hell."

Senior waited as Junior processed.

"I don't think I'm following…what about Hell?"

"My child, you just left it."

About Janelle Jalbert

Janelle Jalbert is an author with a diverse background. In addition to working as a ghost writer and copywriter she served as a reporter and photographer covering motorsports, locally and nationally for Examiner.com. She began her reporting work in the area of education, covering graduate schools in 2009.

Janelle wrote and published *Success Skills for Middle and High School Students* (2001) and was a chapter contributor in *Conscious Entrepreneurs* (2008). Janelle wrote the soon-to-be-released *Wine for Beginners* from For Beginners Publishing. She continues to write novels and fiction that incorporate mystical, paranormal, and metaphysical elements in various genres.

In addition to writing, Janelle taught for more than a decade. She taught English and education courses at the university level, and English in middle schools and high schools in the Los Angeles area.

When she's not writing, Janelle enjoys traveling, racing, and embracing life. She can be found enjoying a glass of wine and hanging with her pups when she's not locked to her computer or exploring the crazy world in which we live.

Janelle currently resides in Southern California but regularly escapes to North Carolina.

Connect with Janelle Jalbert
Twitter: @JustJJWriting
Facebook:
www.facebook.com/janellejalbert.author
Webpage: www.janellejalbert.com

About Synchron8 Publishing

Janelle Jalbert is one of the authors associated with Synchron8 Publishing. We are part micro-publisher and part author- collective, supporting those who have a passion for the written word in its various forms. Our authors work together to create pieces of their own as well as to help promote the works of others. Writers benefit from Synchron8 Publishing resources whether they decide to self-publish or to go a more conventional publishing route.

Our catalogue includes: cookbooks, informational books, non-fiction, and various types of fiction. Learn more at:

www.synchron8publishing.com

We hope you enjoyed the flash fiction of Janelle Jalbert's *Life's Moments*. If you did, please take a moment to leave a review, to help others enjoy it too, wherever you purchased this collection. If you haven't downloaded your free, bonus stories as our thank you, please visit:

www.synchron8publishing.com/F40MomentsBonus

About the Flash 40 Anthologies

Flash 40: Life's Moments is the first in a series of collections to promote flash literature. Some collections are entirely fiction while other anthologies will feature flash memoirs or a combination of fiction and non-fiction. All stories in the Flash Series are 1,000 words or less. Collections are based on an overall theme which ties the individual pieces together. Upcoming *Flash 40* and *Flash 14* collections are a combination of single and multi-author endeavors. Anthologies are planned for release twice a year to start, with the ultimate goal of four times per year.

You Can Be the Next Flash 40 Author!

Flash 40: Life's Moments is the first in a series of flash literature collections to be published by Synchron8 Publishing. We are conducting a contest and open call for the next *Flash 40* installment. We are looking for masterpieces in 1,000 words or less for our next collection which is due to be released in summer 2015. Those selected for inclusion will be eligible for a publishing contract for an upcoming *Flash 40* book all of their own.

The official announcement will be made regarding the *Flash 40* contest and open call on January 15, 2015. For the opportunity to learn about the *Flash 40* contest before the official announcement and to receive updates, sign up for our newsletter at:

www.synchron8publishing.com/Flash40Contest